Roustabout

▲

Roustabout

▲

a fiction by
MICHELLE CHALFOUN

HarperCollins*Publishers*

Lyrics from "Tom Traubert's Blues" by Tom Waits
© 1976 by Fifth Floor Music, Inc. Permission Granted.

HarperCollins books may be purchased for educational, business, or sales promotional use. For information please write: Special Markets Department, HarperCollins Publishers, Inc., 10 East 53rd Street, New York, NY 10022.

FIRST EDITION

Designed by Nancy Singer

ISBN 0-06-017297-5

96 97 98 99 00 ❖/HC 10 9 8 7 6 5 4 3 2 1

To everyone who loved me when I didn't
love myself

Acknowledgments

▲

Thanks to Carole Hedges, for giving me the idea to write, and to Tim Tomlinson for teaching me how. Thanks to Robin Hall for reading so many drafts, and all the other "recidivists" for their patient input.

Thanks to Doug Stumpf and Jeff Seroy for the Old Chatham Fiction Writers Workshop. This book wouldn't exist if it didn't exist. And thanks to all the faculty and writers there that first year, for all their continued support.

Big thanks to Mary Evans for her faith and hard work, and to Jenny Lee for the same.

Thanks to Diane Reverand for giving me this chance, and to Robert Jones for his encouraging words.

Thanks, of course, to my family, who are in no way represented in this book—so nobody'd better be stopping the folks in the deli and asking them if any of this *really* happened.

A special thanks to Jimmy M., for saving my life in and out of the circus, for remembering, and for finding me when I was disappearing.

Finally, thanks to Spirit and all my relations.

Contents

▲

Roustabout

▲

Leaving Home

▲

These are my earliest memories:

Ma dancing; feathers and sequins, mirrors and spangles catching and throwing multicolored sparkles on dark-suited men. I hide under a table, picking at the hard sculpture of gum: gray, pink, and green. Powder, lipstick, and rouge applied to my face by gentle hands with long, shiny fingernails. A mirror surrounded by soft lightbulbs. Beautiful women joking, smoking, putting my hair up in diamond clips.

A red and purple sign flashing over the stage. Ma would spell it out, my pointer finger gripped in her hand, tracing the neon letters: "Big *F,* little *o,* triple big *X X X,* small *y.*" A red cartoon fox, in a bikini and lipstick, wrapped its tail around the *y.*

Ma counting dollars, piles of dollars. Every night, one was folded into a bird. I got to keep the ones folded into birds.

"A crane," Ma said.

"What's a crane?"

"A good luck bird," she answered.

I had my own bedroom, back then. I lined the cranes along my windowsill, from one pink curtain to the other. My window faced a river. In the summer, people floated down that river on inner tubes. They'd smile and wave to Ma and me when they passed. We'd be on our porch drinking lemonade. We always waved back. Ma promised when I got big enough we'd float down that river too. But we left before then.

Dishes and cups and vases of glass filled our cabin. Some shimmered like the rainbows in a soap bubble. Some were flat peach or mint green. Some were red fading to yellow. Our house shined with them.

"Depression glass," Ma said. "They'll be worth something someday. I'm gonna leave them all to you."

But we left them behind when we moved. Ma said they'd break in traveling. We left the quilts and most everything else behind, too.

Saturdays we took car rides to the flea market to buy these beautiful things we'd later leave behind. I loved those sunny, buzzing mornings. They smelled like hay and sweet grass. Sometimes someone played a guitar or a fiddle. I ate fried dough with powder sugar on top. I ran from table to table, drunk on the gee-gaws. That's what Ma called everything, gee-gaws and trinkets and doo-dads.

One Saturday, when Ma and me drove to the flea market field, the tables weren't there. Instead the field was crowded with trailers and tents. From the center of the colorful jumble rose a huge tent, the size of a building. It took my breath away. I tugged Ma to the yellow metal fence surrounding this magic place. I fitted my toes and fingers in the fence holes, pressed my body against it. I wanted in.

Ma said, "You ever see a circus?"

"No. Can we go in?" I begged.

"We'll see." She dragged me back to the car. I scuffed my feet and looked over my shoulder the whole way.

That night a new man came to watch Ma dance. He sat in the front row. He came back the next night. They drank coffee for a long time after closing. The chairs were up on the other tables, and the floor was swept around them, and still Ma talked to the circus man. I waited on a barstool, eating the fruit and olives. I played pickup sticks with the cocktail stirrers.

The man had large feet and hands, a large nose, large ears, and a big belt buckle. But his hair, arms, legs, and chest were skinny. At first Ma called him Enis and made me call him Uncle. Later, when we moved in with him, she made me call him Pa.

On the third night, he slipped two red tickets into Ma's waistband.

The next morning, she dressed me up and we went to the show.

In my memories, the colors of the circus are bright like Charms lollipops. Lime green grass, lemon yellow fence, cherry red flags, grape flavored blue tent. Sometimes, when the light's just right, or the lot's been washed clean by a light rain, I can still see it this way. But that day, my senses weren't clouded by reality. I just figured this was heaven, or at least very magic. Candy floss was sweeter than fried dough. The women under the tent did more than dance. They flew through the air, rode elephants, turned double back flips and landed on the shoulders of strong handsome men. I liked that the houses had wheels, that the animals dressed in fancy clothes. Tiny booths with balloons and dolls tempted me. When Ma asked me if I'd like to live there, I said yes. I didn't understand that meant leaving home.

At home, Ma rushed around. She threw my backpack at me; she said, "Fill this with toys. It's all we have room for." I filled it with the dollar cranes and my Calico Bear. She was tearing through the house, opening drawers, tossing clothes into bags.

She ran back into my room. "The dollars, where are they?" she yelled. I unzipped my backpack and showed her. She grabbed it, up-ended it, dumped it out. Dollar cranes fluttered to the floor. She scared me.

"Shit," she cursed. "Unfold them." Her hands worked furiously. She tore one. "Fuck, shit. Don't tear any, Matty." I was crying now. "Okay, sweetie?" She softened a bit. She rubbed at my tears with the hem of her shirt. "You be my helper. Mama's little helper. You're my good girl, right?"

Then she took her seam ripper and opened Calico Bear's back. "Don't, don't!" I wailed.

"I'll sew him back," she said. "This is for our secret treasure. Can you keep a secret?" I nodded. I wanted to be brave. She put my unfolded crane dollars in a roll with her own savings. She stuffed this, rubber-banded, inside Bear's body. She sewed long, hasty stitches, worrying under her breath. "Oh God, let us make it. Oh please oh please oh please please."

It was dark, past time for work. The phone rang. "Don't pick that up!" she screamed. She yanked the cord from the wall.

When Calico Bear was sewed, she thrust him in my arms. We drove fast to catch the circus before it moved on.

Years later, Ma would take the bear from my sleeping arms and pick the stitches from his back. She'd take the secret treasure money roll and she'd leave. The bear would be in my arms the next morning, seams open, stuffing trailing to the floor. But Ma would be gone.

June
1984

▲

How I Pay

▲

While the rest of the circus sleeps, Jack Diamond, the fancy-trick roper, whips Marlboros from his wife Brandy's bruised and trembling lips.

They rehearse under the empty bigtop. While it's still early morning cool, before Tattoo Lou heats it up with horse practice, before Jay bosses his ringcrew to set the props and rake ringdirt.

Brandy is chained to the brightly scrolled bandstand. The wrist and ankle cuffs are plastic, painted to look like iron. Jack stalks around the ring, flashing malice and venom from his milky eyes. She's perfected a facial expression that reads of courage in the face of certain doom, even from the last row of the side grandstand. And he looks menacing and dangerous, twirling the rattlesnake whip over his thinning hair.

A sharp crack. A shower of sparks. Suddenly, miraculously, Brandy's lips are empty. Feigned openmouthed surprise from her, triumphant grin from him. He holds two halves of a neatly broken cigarette to his imagined audience. His hands will stop trembling by the matinee. He bows, he styles to his wife. She nods and smiles graciously at the empty bleachers. Her skin is pitted with tiny white pinholes. A thousand divots from fallen ash. Heavy pancake allows her to still get away with a low-cut gown. Her large chest, heaving with pretend fear, has always been one of the act's best assets. Some things never change.

Every morning, I wake to the crack of Jack's rattlesnake whip. I could be sweating alone in the top bunk of my sleeper, or comfortable in the double-wide bed of Jayson's Country Squire. My hips cradled inside his, my shoulders pressed against his warm chest, his arm heavy and reassuring across my breasts.

Crack. My eyes open.

Jayson's wall clock reads 6:25. Already too hot. The green dish towel he uses as a curtain has slipped from the rod. Hot white sunlight littered with dust bakes my side of the bed. Half aroused, he rolls my nipple between his thumb and finger. I stretch onto my back. We shift in familiar ways. Then I'm beneath him. He kisses my eyelids. Nose. Chin. My fingers play down the bumps of his spine. Outside, the birds are already lulled to silence by the heat. Though the air is still and breezeless, sounds drift in: Al fixing breakfast in the cookhouse, banging pots, running water. Someone cursing quietly from sleeper row. And the smells: salt grease of old popcorn, garlic-rot of hotdogs decomposing under the bleachers, vinyl coated canvas delaminating in the heat, elephant, horse, unwashed crew.

Jayson slides his tongue from one breast to the other. Like he's licking an envelope, without thinking what's inside.

I wonder when my life will change.

For over three years now, since my fifteenth birthday,
I've been coming to Jayson's trailer. He knows my body so
well his movements seem automatic. The same concentration as when he lubes his Harley. He works from the top
down. Lips, tits, clit, in. My body still responds. I shouldn't
complain. He kisses each of my ribs. Brown curls brush my
skin.

So if there are fifty-two weeks in a year, and we do it on
average three or four times a week, that would be 3.5 times
52, then that times 3 years; but then there's a half year
more. I give up on the math and roll my eyes to the pressboard trailer walls instead.

Before Jayson in the Country Squire, there was Pa in the
Airstream for six years. This began the night after Ma ran
off. I was nine. He started slow at first, just a finger, then
two. Then three. I don't remember exactly when Pa finally
made me bleed. All I know is I didn't bleed just the first
time. When I lay under Pa my head would bang against this
one pressboard wall. If I tilted my head and rolled my eyes
upward, I could watch the wall give a little with each thrust.
A nailhead pushed its way out of the cheap pulp siding, and
I watched it, imagined it working its way out a bit more
each time my forehead banged against the wall. I made bets
with myself: Who would fall out first, Pa or the nail? I
remember trying mental telepathy. I'd chant in my head,
"Out ... Out ... " The nailhead was still there when I
packed my things and changed trailers.

Soon after my fifteenth birthday, Jayson noticed me
hanging out wash behind Pa's silver-bullet Airstream.
Perhaps he'd been sniffing around before; I remember his
eyes sliding off my body when I looked up quickly in the
cookhouse. Not like I'd have much chance to notice; Pa had
threatened every crew member individually—if anyone

touched his daughter, he'd cut off his balls and sew them shut in his mouth with seine twine.

Jayson is handsome in a way Pa wasn't. Jay is solid and confident; Pa was skinny and slippery. Pa never looked other men in the eye; Jay stares them down and bosses them around. Staying with Pa made me feel so dirty. Jayson is the ringcrew chief. I used to believe his protection would keep my name clean in all the gossips' mouths.

Later, Jayson told me he knew all along he could take Pa out, so he wasn't afraid. Defiant, he stood right outside Pa's Airstream and said "Hi." I said it back.

He walked around to me and lifted my sweaty hair off my neck. "You sure got beautiful hair," he said. I thought he was teasing; he could see it needed a wash. Then he lifted a torn pocket tee out the basket and pinned it to the line. We lifted a stained sheet together, his hand on one corner and mine on the other.

"You know, it doesn't have to be like this." He jutted his chin at a yellow stain.

"Bleach won't get them out. I tried."

He laughed. "I'm not talking about laundry." He kicked the bumper where Pa had put a sticker that said: "Don't come a-knockin' if the trailer's a-rockin'."

"That's none of your business." I snatched the wet sheet off the line and balled it up, threw it back in the basket.

He picked it out and hung it again. "You know I got my own trailer now."

"Congratulations. Hope you enjoy it."

"I'd enjoy it better with company." He clipped a clothespin on my tee-shirt, right above my heart.

I used it to hang a pair of Pa's briefs. "I don't know you well enough for that."

He laughed again. "Well, I'll move you in with Al. He'll play chaperon, till we get to know each other well enough."

I ran through the Airstream, stuffing my things into a garbage bag while Pa and Jayson squared off out front. I even took the bedspread, because I had sewed it. I was careful to leave nothing behind, except the pink plastic flamingos with their skinny steel legs stuck in the front lawn; I knew how much Pa hated them.

Eventually Pa and Jayson took to swinging at each other, and a crowd gathered, roustabouts and performers mingling in a way that only happens during fights. Jayson, clearly stronger, brought Pa to his knees. His ringcrew cheered him on. "She'll be rockin' Jay's trailer now!" I stepped out the trailer to the protection of Jayson's armpit. The performer wives pretended to be weakened by the sight of Pa's bleeding lip. They covered their eyes with clean manicured hands. They spoke quiet French and Italian, as if chatting about the weather and the small audiences, as if they weren't standing in front of Pa's trailer, waiting, watching.

I walked through the crowd slow and graceful, like I was walking around the ring styling my costume. Tom, the canvas boss, held Pa at the elbows. Even so, Pa was shaking a sledgehammer handle and screaming at me, "You're gonna pay, you ungrateful bitch! You're gonna pay!"

Jay carried my bags to Al's sleeper. Al kissed me on both cheeks. "Sugar-booger, this is the girlfriends' sleeper now. We gonna have fun; just like sisters." To celebrate our sisterhood, he made cocktails out of champagne and raspberry liquor, and I swore never to live with another straight man again.

Now I was no longer supported by Pa, I had to work. I started in the costume truck with Tante. Sewing sequins back on leotards, patching fishnets worn down between the thighs by elephant hair. We disguised old costumes with feathers and tulle. We turned Tattoo Lou's horses into unicorns with satin-covered cardboard cones. Outside, the costume truck was bright white, painted with gold and red curlicues: *Fabrizio's Circus Fantastico*. Inside, it was damp wood walls with metal supports; bungee cords holding washers and dryers and racks of musty costumes. Buttons and rhinestones and ribbons, tangles of rich fabrics mildewing in the damp. I hated the dark cave, sitting all day. I'd grumble and Tante would scold. "Suffering is good for the soul. Jesus hung on the cross for three days until he died. Now he sits at the right hand of God. You should be so lucky." She'd stroke her yellow nails along the crinkled tissue of her burn-scarred skin. "You don't know what is suffering." She'd point to the eye patch covering her empty left socket. I knew she knew suffering. I knew she'd seen more with her one eye than most with two. She could tell me everything my ma never did.

Still, on moves, I wanted to be outside, on top of the tent instead of folding sweat-stained costumes into bubble wrap. Before Jay's fight with Pa, Tom would take me up the laceline and sit me next to him on top of the mast, between the flags. He'd always spread his arms out like he owned the sky. "Best seat in the house," he'd say. Under the big-top, we'd swing the quarterpole ropes round these heavy steel supports like fliers on trapeze. Setting up the tent was all energy and power. I wanted to be high in the air, legs wrapped around the mast, callus ripping on ropes and cables. I wanted to ride the bucking canvas, to wrestle it against the wind, lacing it tight, secure. I could tie all the knots, I could carry sidepoles on my shoulder, a hundred without dropping. I yelled "Hit it back!" loud as any man;

and I could guy out the tent exactly, till it snapped into a perfect circle, tight as a drumskin. I tried to convince Tom to let me on the tent crew.

Tom said, "No openings."

"You could fit me in." I stomped around, hands on hips. "You taught me everything yourself. You know I'm good. It's 'cause I'm a girl."

He looked over my head. "It's 'cause you're Enis's girl. Wait till he calms down."

I didn't have to wait long. In his anger, Pa had been drinking round the clock, even during moves. He got meaner and sloppier, off balance all the time. Two weeks after I moved out, Pa fell off the top of the tent. I was sitting at the door of the costume truck, beading a cape, wishing I was up there, rigging. Pa's feet slipped out from under him. He hollered. I dropped my needle. Pa slid down the laceline, his yellow rainsuit slick on the plastic-coated canvas. When he hit the ground, his screams stopped short, like someone clicked off a radio mid-song. Tom, Jayson, and me leaned over his twisted body. A three foot round pool of blood circled his head, split wide open on a stake. Tom lifted Pa's wrist. Checked for a pulse. Pa's fingers fell back at unnatural angles. I figured he broke them grabbing at laces along the way, trying to stop his fall.

I pulled a Lucky from behind my ear and took Tom's lighter right out his pocket.

"You got an opening now," I said.

At Pa's funeral, the minister gave us a moment to remember Pa out loud. Damp wind blew through the thin cotton dress Al had lent me. We'd stuffed the toes of his black pumps with newspaper so they'd fit me, and now the heels sank into the muddy cemetery lawn. The minister cleared his throat.

Tom dropped his eyes to his boots. "Enis always worked hard."

Jay squeezed my hand. "We had our differences," he said.

Al touched his handkerchief to the corners of his dry eyes. "Excuse me." He blew his nose loudly.

Tante muttered in Arabic and made crosses over the grave.

I had nothing to say that should be said of the dead. I might've said, "Serves you right, bastard." I could've spit, "Ma and me were fine before you came along." I wanted to yell at the minister, "What the fuck you looking at?" But he didn't seem to want to be there any more than the rest of us. No performers had showed. Not even Tattoo Lou, though once she'd been tight with Ma, years ago. Ringmaster Fabrizio didn't even come. I just threw my handful of dirt on the casket. It thudded.

Jay and me stopped at a bar before going home. I had lots of Wild Turkeys. Jay bought them. The bartender never carded me. We drank and held hands across the booth. We followed overgrown train tracks back to the lot. I balance beam walked on the rail and he steadied me.

That night was our first time. After sex, my damp skin cooled except where we still touched. Jay smelled like bourbon, tobacco, and fresh dirt after rain. He kissed me everywhere for what seemed like hours. I felt like I knew why I was supposed to be alive. When I woke the next morning he was still holding me.

Back at the sleeper, Al shook his head. "Child, a man don't buy the cow when he gets the milk free."

I hung his dress back in his closet and changed into Carhartts. "I told Jay I won't move in with him till he marries me."

"You'll be waiting a long time, Girlfriend," Al said.

Over three years later, I'm still waiting.

Jayson finishes with my clit. I know what's next. I ask, "You got condoms?"

He stops moving over me and looks up.

"Shit, I forgot," he says.

He hovers there, thinking for a moment. Then he reaches over to the shelf and takes down some Corn Huskers lotion.

He knows I don't like it this way; it hurts more. But he's told me many times how it feels better. And he doesn't have to worry about getting me pregnant.

"Do you mind?" he asks. We know I won't refuse.

I shrug and roll over on my hands and knees. I think about relaxing. I concentrate on my breath. I look at the pressboard wall for exposed nailheads. When that doesn't work, I reach between my legs to hurry things along.

Later, in the Porta-John, I make a mental note to buy condoms. I picture attaching the note to my watch, just like Tom taught me. When I see my watch, I'll remember to go down the road to the drugstore.

In a perfect set-up, 152 stakes support the external structure of the bigtop: 120 spaced equally around the tent, one at each sidepole, plus four extra at each of the six lace-lines, plus eight for the backstage extension. Each should hold equal tension, pulling the tent into a perfectly round circle. If any section weakens, even one stake, the bigtop's in danger.

No set-up is perfect. The ground's never completely level, and stakes pull from rain softened dirt. It's my job to watch the stakes for signs of weakness. I walk around the tent, inspecting for loose stakes that need backstaking, a second or third stake rigged to them for support. Tom thinks he taught me the proper way to drive stakes, but actually, Pa did. When I find a stake that's pulling, I measure the hole with my fingers. If two or more fingers fit in the hole with the stake, I drop one or more stakes, depending on what the hole needs, and a length of rope on the ground to mark it.

I walk back around the tent a second time, now with a 16-pound sledge, looking for those guylines where I preset more stakes and rope. I hold the new stake behind the old, at a slight angle so the head leans away from the tent, and tap it in place with short jerky taps, hand up near the head of the sledge. Then I stand up and back. Slide my hands to the end of the sledge handle, right hand above the left. Left leg forward, right leg back. Size up the swing with a slow practice arc. "This is important," Pa would say. "If you don't size up your swing, you may hit the stake with the wood and ruin a perfectly good handle."

I get my mark. The hammer swings down past my knees, up and around over my shoulders, and back down onto the stake. This full circle lets the sledge do the work. I can bury a stake with six strokes. Pa, who could do it in three, used to stand there counting my strokes. "Not bad for a girl," he'd say, "but not good enough."

Once, I heard him yelling at a new crew, "You a bunch of lazy-ass, First-of-May suckin'-on-your-mama's-teats New-Jacks! My little girl can drive stakes better one-handed." Some roustabout whose name I forgot or never even knew cracked, "What else can she do one-handed?" Pa laid him out with the sledgehammer handle. When he came to, Tom ran him off the lot. This still makes me smile whenever I think on it. I tie the first stake off to the backstake, smiling.

This work makes me proud. I like the way the sledge feels, I like the sound of the hammer on the stakes, and I like working alone. I feel strong, important. Sometimes I wish I could drive stakes all day, every day.

Back in the tent truck, I lean against the wall between the bent stakes and the fresh coils of yellow poly-pro. A cigarette. A chance to catch my breath. I rub my work warmed hands together, pleased with the thickness of my fingers, the hardness of my palms.

Between moves, it's my job to maintain the canvas. Open and close the tent for shows. Today I'm supposed to cut new lines for the horse tent. Looking for the heat gun, I run my eyes along the wall. Grommet kit, come-alongs, seine twine, and tieline. There's the hot-glue kit and Tom's ditty bag. My eyes fall on my watch. Condoms, I think. I'll do the lines later, during the show.

I check my pockets. A dollar and some change.

Back at the sleeper, I grab a fistful of pennies from Al's change drawer and my jacket off the bed. The wind has changed; it's cooled off some. Tom taught me to keep an eye on the weather; says weather knowledge is important for good tent management. Doesn't look like storm clouds. I slam the blue and red sleeper door shut, hop over the yellow security fence, and run towards town.

At the drugstore, I stare at the condom display. Naturlamb. Rough Rider, Ribbed for Her Pleasure. Hot Cinnamon. Wet 'n Wild. All hung on the wall behind the counter. I'll have to ask the old lady at the register to get me some. She is chicken skinny; her store apron collapses into her deflated chest. I can't read the price on any of them. I'm squinting at the prices when the lady says, "You decide?"

"Well, how much is the cheapest?" I meet her eyes.

"You can get a pack of three non-lubed Trojans for a buck fifty, but your boyfriend'll hate you when he's trying to put the damn thing on." I wonder how this dried up old prune could have such knowledge. And I wonder why she'd tell me. She probably gets off talking about condoms. Freak.

"Now, what I suggest is your reservoir tip with the nonoxynol-9 lubrication." She reaches for a black and gold box with two lovers walking into a sunset. "Pack of three for a dollar eighty-nine, the best you can get for that money." The box sits on the counter, and I read the gold script: For That Feeling of Love.

"Yeah, well, I'll take those. Whatever you just said." I start counting out change from my hand to the counter.

The chicken lady counts along with her eyes, and says, "All change?"

"No, there's a dollar." I lay the wrinkled bill on the counter along with the change. Jesus. Like it matters how I pay.

"Well, a girl's gotta pay for her fun somehow." She drops the box into a small brown bag and rings up my purchase. "Gotta protect herself." She titters into her hand, then touches her hair lightly, patting it like she just found a poodle resting on her head. I can't get out of there fast enough. The spongy mat in front of the door sings "Bing-bong," announcing my exit. The "bong" cuts off sharply.

Outside, the bright sun sparkles off the green and brown glass embedded in the street. Like Tante has come through and hot-glued rhinestones to the asphalt. The clouds have blown off, but the breeze has picked up. I'm glad to have my jacket. The air smells suburban. Cut grass, pool chlorine, backyard cookout charcoal. I consider wandering around town a bit, maybe buying myself a soda and a magazine. Then I realize I don't have any more money. Still, I could sit on a green wooden bench and watch people. I could window shop. Or even wander through the stores, touching things. Take clothes off the rack and hold them against my body, hanger and all. When the store ladies ask me if I need help, or even look at me funny, I could say, "I'm just browsing," like Ma used to when we went out shopping together. If I found a beautiful dress, I'd buy it, and wear it home so Jayson would see how pretty I look. He'd tell me I was beautiful, and he'd maybe ask me out. We could go to dinner, or go dancing. At the end of the evening, he'd drop me off at my sleeper door and we'd kiss good night. Like a real date.

A dummy in the window of Young Miss Fashions wears a flowered dress with fabric so light it's nearly see-through. It would float when I walked. The square of cardboard hanging from the sleeve says $78. A woman looks through the dusty window at me. Her fingers rest lightly on the window dress. Our eyes meet. One thick nickel warms in my palm. I decide I don't really want to be inside, shopping. It's too beautiful out. Warm in the sun and cool in the shade. I consider walking up and down the side streets, looking at the houses and the yards, wondering about the families inside.

Instead I keep on walking along the main street, past the school and onto the main road. Where the houses and stores end, the road begins to look like an interstate, except for the flowers on the median strip. I walk with traffic, even though the circus lot is on the other side of the street. It's down a ways, about a half mile, and there's no sidewalk on that side of the road. Just a thin strip of grass and a tall twist wire fence. The steel wire forms diamond-shaped holes.

I walk slowly, enjoying the air, eyes fixed on the white

and blue tent in the distance. Bright flags wave in the breeze. I'd go to that show if I lived in town. I think of kids coming home from school clutching free tickets the 24-hour man passed out at recess, that scrap of red cardboard nearly melting in their hot wet hands. Begging their folks over suppers of pork chops and collard greens, "Can we go please?" The folks give in and buy five more tickets for the rest of the family, just because the advance man gave little Suzie a free one while she hung from the monkey bars.

I wonder what Al's making for lunch and whether Tom has any projects for this afternoon. Straightening stakes maybe? Probably those horse tent lines. If not, maybe I could come back into town and do me and Jayson's laundry. He'd give me quarters. Maybe Al would come too.

A red van slows down beside me. "Hey, circus lady."

I almost flinch, but I recover before my body gives me away. I keep walking. Except for a small sideways flick out the corner of my eye, I ignore the two guys waving at me.

"Hey, are you the lion tamer? You want to tame my lion, lady?" The guy on the passenger side is leaning out the window and banging his hand against the door of the van.

"You know how to charm a cobra?" I wonder how they know I'm from the show. Then I realize I'm wearing my tour jacket. My face goes hot, armpits sticky. I'd take off my jacket, but I don't want to carry it. Pa taught me in such a situation I should always keep my hands free.

"Maybe she's a freak." "Yeah, are you the freak? You got three tits or something?" They're both talking and laughing now, inching along at my pace.

Cars honk and pass them; they're stopping traffic. They look about 20, 21; one guy has dark hair. The van inches along so close I'm sure the dark haired guy could touch my left shoulder if he leaned out the window a bit. I move onto the grass. It would be stupid to run, I think. Goddamn townies.

"Freak me, baby." My heart stalls, restarts a moment later with a loud thump. Sweaty palms stain the paper bag.

"Freak me, baby." "Freak me, fuck." "Fuck me, freak." My skin tightens. They're so loud. Stop. Please stop, I want to scream.

"Fuck me, you fuckin' freak!"

I duck behind the van. Run across the street. A pickup shoots past my hips, the driver cursing me. I feel better now that they are on the other side of the road. Still, I find myself trying to walk quickly, but the grass strip beside the fence is narrow; my feet stumble a little, kicking up divots. I stare into oncoming traffic. The cars and trucks drive towards, then past me, a foot from my shoulder.

Across the road, the red van picks up speed again, moves with traffic. I watch it drive away. Up ahead there's a break in the median strip. The red van pulls a U-turn through the break and heads back towards me. I think: They can't do anything but drive by; I'm facing oncoming traffic, what can they do?

The red van pulls up alongside me and stops. A blue sedan honks and swerves around them, its driver yelling something I don't hear.

"Hey, mama, don't be so cold. You aren't being very nice now, are you?" The passenger talks at me while the driver concentrates on driving backwards and slow. They'll get tired of this fast, I think. Just don't look, I think. My focus sharpens. Unnecessary images disappear. I concentrate on the tent getting larger, too slowly. My vision narrows to only the tent and the van.

"She's not being very nice, is she, Jack? My mama says circus people aren't nice, says they live like animals. You like an animal?" He growls at me, then barks. The hairs on my neck and forearms raise off my skin. Like a dog's.

Another car drives around them, laying on the horn. Where are all the highway cops?

"I wanna teach you how to be nice, circus lady." The dark-haired passenger opens the door. The edge hits my shoulder. My mind goes blank. My body becomes a machine.

Fence. Muscles snap. I throw my bag over the top and stick my toes and fingers through the diamond shaped holes. Kick the hand reaching for my ankle and grab for the silver twist-tops of the fence. Don't listen to the dark haired one yelling. Swinging my left leg over, I feel my jeans catch, then rip.

When I bend down to pick up my bag, I hear, "That bitch is crazy. Let's get outta here."

The drugstore bag is very red. I look at my right hand; it's very red too. The pinkie has fallen away from the bone. Yellow globs of fat fall past the red and white gristle to the grass. There is yellow fat in my hand. Where is the pain? So much blood . . .

Blood.

Time slows. A lightness fills my head. The silver fence glitters and shines. Tears on my eyelashes draw a rainbow halo around the distant tent. I don't feel like I'm crying, yet there are tears dropping. But I feel just fine, like I'm floating. When I get to the tent, everything will be okay.

I tuck the bag in my pocket with my clumsy left hand and then wrap this left hand around the bloody right one. It registers that the flesh is all there, just sliced neatly, peeled back like a banana skin. I put pressure on my hand and hold both over my head. My feet skim the ground. I'm flying towards the lot. I don't look back to see if the townies are still there.

"Just breathe, keep breathing." Jayson looks over at me so often I worry he'll drive off the road. I lean my head against the cool glass of the Suburban. My hand's raised above my heart, propped up on the dashboard.

He says, "Shit, Mat, how're you gonna work now? That was stupid, real stupid." I don't know what kind of answer he wants.

"What exactly happened?"

"Some guys were bugging me on the road, so I went over the fence." I close my eyes.

"Hey now, hey. Don't go to sleep. Keep breathing. Tell me what happened." He looks over at me again. Maybe he is worried.

"They were following me in their van."

"So why didn't you cross the road?"

"I did, but they did too. They drove backwards, against traffic, to keep yelling at me." I really can't explain this, I think. Already it makes no sense to me.

"Did they touch you? Did the fuckers touch you? I swear . . . " He tries to think of something he can do. Make them pay. For a moment my eyes tear up. I blink and then stare at the continuous white line of guardrail streaming past my window.

"No, I got over the fence. My hand just got caught on those twisty wires on top is all." I feel kind of cold.

"You okay?" Jayson looks at me again. It takes me a while to answer, so he asks again.

"I'm fine. A little cold is all." I want to lie down. Instead I say, "I'm glad Tom gave us the production vehicle. I don't think I could've stayed on your motorcycle. Tom's so nice . . . "

"Yes, he's nice."

"You're nice too." My voice is sleepy.

"Yes, I'm nice too." He looks over at me, and I smile back slowly.

"I'm nice too, Jayson." I feel very nice.

"You're nice too, Matty." He looks at me. His forehead is wrinkled in a way that makes him look old and sad.

"Don't look so worried. I can't feel my hand now. It doesn't hurt anymore."

"That's good, that's good. You're gonna be fine, fine."

"Fine."

"Don't go to sleep now."

"No, I'm fine," I say. I feel fine. Numb.

"How are you going to pay?" The secretary nurse shuffles papers. She's all in white. She has many forms for us to fill out before they'll take me in.

"Don't know." I don't know if I said that out loud or not. I feel cold again. Sleepy. Stay awake, look around. On the wall a poster shows a naked woman in profile. Her body is see-through, her internal organs covered with layers of fat. Fat coats her body. The artist colored the fat yellow, and it looks just like what fell out my finger. The heading reads: "Fat, the Leading Cause of Today's Health Problems."

"Workman's comp. She got workman's comp from the circus. Where's your wallet, honey?" Jayson starts feeling in my jacket pockets.

"In my back pocket, silly." I giggle. I feel his hand in my pocket, and that makes me giggle more.

"Name?" the nurse asks. Pen taps the clipboard. She doesn't seem to like her job much.

"That's Jayson," I tell her.

She looks disgusted. Or bored. "No, ma'am. I mean you, the patient."

"Oh, sorry." I want to know when we're going to leave. I don't feel so great. I want to go to sleep. "I want to go to sleep," I tell Jayson, but he isn't listening, he's talking to the nurse.

"Listen, lady, can we do something here? My girlfriend's in shock or something. She could lose that finger. Just get her a doctor and I'll fill out any goddamn form you want."

"You called me your girlfriend. He called me his girl-friend," I tell the nurse.

Jay brushes his knuckles across my forehead. Tucks my hair behind my ears. "You're my girl, aren't you?" He's star-ing at the wall behind the nurse. He answers himself. "You're my girl."

The nurse secretary flips around the clipboard and points to a line with an X. "Okay, just as long as she signs here."

I try to pick up the pen, but my right hand isn't work-ing. My left hand's stuck to it. I try again, but I can't seem to separate my hands. Instead I start to cry. "I can't sign it, Jayson, I can't. What's wrong with my hand?"

"Here now. Nothing's wrong." He lays his hand on top of my two stuck together hands and helps me make an X.

"There, you happy now?" The clipboard scuttles across her desk, scattering pens, papers. I don't see why Jayson is being so mean to the nurse.

"Why are you being so mean?" I call back over my shoulder. A large man in white leads me down the hall.

The male nurse sits me down. His hands are heavy on my shoulders. "Where's Jayson? I need Jayson here."

He doesn't answer. He plunges my hand in a basin of yellow disinfectant. My hands come apart, and I scream.

*   *   *

Later, cops show up on the lot. One older, heavier; one young, blond, and slim. I meet them in the cookhouse with Jayson. Al offers us all coffee. He takes extra time pouring the younger cop's cup. He sings, "I love a man in uniform," lightly under his breath. I stare at the white gauze bandage on my hand, waiting for something to begin. My pinkie has 21 stitches; I wonder if I can take them out myself, or if I'll have to go back to a hospital.

"Well, ma'am, do you want to press charges?" This comes from the young blond cop. He has a notebook and pen. The older cop concentrates on rolling a Drum cigarette. The young cop doesn't look much older than 18. He can't be much older than me.

"Yeah, we want those bastards to pay. Look what they did to Mat here." Jayson points at my hand. It looks impressive with so much bandage.

"She works with her hands, you know; she's a rigger," Al calls from his corner.

"Who's this?" asks the older cop. He licks the paper to seal his cigarette.

"My sleeper mate," I say. Al winks at the young blond. The older cop grunts and spits a thread of tobacco.

"Well, Nelly"—he glances towards Al and smiles at his young partner—"that's something for lawyers, later, if you sue. We only deal with relevant facts."

"Any witnesses?" The young cop's pen hovers over his clipboard.

I think of the cars that drove by without stopping. "No," I answer.

"Just exactly what happened?" He lifts his pen again.

"Well, they were following me in their van and yelling things at me, so I crossed the street to get away. They pulled a U-turn and started driving backwards against traffic in order to continue bothering me."

"What do you mean by bothering, exactly?" The young cop hasn't written anything yet.

"You know, like 'Hey, baby' and whatnot." I don't feel like getting into it for these guys.

"Did they touch you?" The old cop asks this.

"Well, the passenger got out the van . . . "

"Yes, but were you ever touched?" The young one only writes now, the older one asking all the questions.

"Only by the van door."

"So no one ever touched you?"

"No, I got away before they got a chance to."

"So how did you get injured?"

"Climbing over the fence. You know, to get away." I shake a cigarette out of my pack with my left hand, but I don't put it to my lips. Instead I roll it around the table with my bandaged hand.

The cookhouse walls are transparent vinyl. Outside, the concessionaires open up their tents. They concentrate on attaching balloons to strings, fuzzy toy monkeys to sticks. No one looks towards us.

"So those boys did not cut you; you cut yourself by accident, climbing a fence." The old cop finally lights his Drum.

I concentrate on pushing my cigarette around on the table. Eventually I look up and say, "I got cut because I had to climb over the fence fast, to get away. So they wouldn't do anything to me." A few bars of "Rock the Casbah" blast through the air. Sound check. Soon the lot will open to the public.

"Well . . . " The cop sucks his Drum and blows smoke

rings, clicking his jaw once for each ring. "How do we ever know what someone is gonna do, right? I mean, I would think when you take a cigarette out of a pack you're gonna smoke it, but look, here you are just pushing it around the table." He gestures at me with his Drum between his short thumb and forefinger. "Get my point?" he says.

I look at Jayson. I can't believe he isn't saying anything. I pick up the Lucky Strike and clench it between my teeth. Tobacco squeezes out onto my tongue. I talk around it while I search my pockets with my clumsy left hand.

"They threatened me. I know they wanted to do something to me. Isn't that something?" I look at Al, and he sashays over slow to light my cigarette with a coy flick of his lighter. I release a big drag at the old cop.

"Well," says the old cop, "as I see it, some town boys see an attractive circus lady"—his eyes slide across my breasts—"and they want to get to know her. You know you shouldn't walk unaccompanied in a strange town, don't you? And with these two men to protect you . . . " He looks at Al, and the young cop smiles. "What were you doing out by yourself on a Friday morning in a strange town, hmmm?"

Buying condoms, I say to myself.

"Besides, there is no way I can arrest some boys for intent to do something, now can I?"

I sit with my mouth open. When I finally think to shut it, I can hear my teeth come together hard. I wonder if they could hear that outside my mouth. "So you're saying the only way I could press charges would be if they touched me?"

"Well, actually, only if you could prove they touched you in a malicious way. And unfortunately, there were no witnesses." He smiles at the younger cop, no longer pretending to take notes.

"Maybe I should've stood there and let them hurt me so

I'd have a case. But I guess that wouldn't be good enough. I mean, no one stopped to witness." I want to yell this, but I only speak softly.

"Now, ma'am, there's no need to get angry. I realize you're a little hysterical after your scare. But that's all it was. A little scare." He leans forward in his chair and holds his finger and thumb like he's pinching the air. His uniform pants stretch tight across his lap. A small bulge, too far down on his left thigh to make sense, gags me. He follows my eyes. I want to throw hot coffee and watch him shrivel. His hand pats my forearm once. I shake him off.

"What I'm saying is, there's little chance a lady"—he smiles at the young cop—"a lady like yourself would have much of a case against some local boys who were just being friendly."

Jayson straightens up the Country Squire, picking up clothes and smelling them. Some he throws in a green nylon stuff sack, some he folds and puts back in the drawer. I'm sitting on the fold-out bed. Cradling my hurt hand with my good hand. He explains to me that people can get arrested for assault with intent to kill. This I already know, because Tante's husband was arrested for that after he burned her, or so she says. But there is no law against harassment with intent to rape, he continues. At least not here. Not with street encounters . . .

I listen to the rhythm of his words playing against the clown walkabout music. A light roar from the tent. Jacomo has just thrown confetti on the front row; they thought it would be water.

. . . maybe in offices . . . but not on streets . . . free speech . . . take it as a compliment . . .

Jason moves around the trailer, looking for anything he

might have missed. "What were you doing anyhow, Mat? In town, on a show day?"

I think of what Ma used to say: "If he's trying to buy, you must be advertising."

"Hey, Jay," I say under my breath but loud enough for him to hear, "you forgot to say I was asking for it."

He straightens up and drops a shirt from his hands. "Jesus, Mat, whose fault was it? Mine?"

His back twitches. The audience roars.

"You didn't have condoms. I was buying condoms, so maybe you'd face me for once." I wait. Something will happen now.

He turns with his fist raised. Dust sparkles past my eyes on a stream of sunlight. His fist breaks through the shiny particles and sends them dancing away.

Inches from my face, he turns. Hits the wall clock. It shatters. I don't move. The air vibrates around me.

For a long while he stares at the blood on his knuckles.

"I face you." His knuckles are bleeding. His bottom lip is pushed out. "I always face you. The whole time except for that one thing."

I feel so tired. I don't have the energy to argue. Nothing changes.

"Sorry," I say.

"No, I'm sorry."

"It's okay. It's fine," I say.

"It's just this all just makes me so mad." He waves his bloody hand weakly, gesturing at nothing in particular, maybe at everything in general. "And I hate it when you put words in my mouth," he says quietly.

"Sorry."

"Don't say that if you don't mean it."

"No, Jay, I'm really sorry."

"Then why did you say that?"

"Sorry, Jayson; I guess it's just been a hard day."

"Yeah, well, I had to miss ringset to drive you. I was worried. I was worried and I missed ringset. How do you think that made me feel?"

"Sorry, Jayson. Sorry."

I hold myself very still while he washes the blood off his knuckles. He should be in the tent, wearing his tux, directing the ringcrew. But he's here with me. And I really need him here. I really need him to be nice. I need to be held, rocked, touched gently. Anything. Anything to get me out of my head, which keeps replaying the day.

He hands me a Band-Aid and I stretch it across his cut. My bandaged hand feels stiff and fat, and I don't do a good job.

The juggling music begins. His lips move as he counts the acts left in the show. I don't want to be alone.

I say, "Jay, I really want to thank you for taking me to the hospital."

He puts his hand on my knee. "Anytime."

"No, really, thank you," I say again, holding his tee-shirt at the neck with my left hand.

He smiles down at me. I notice his cheeks and lips sag when he leans over, making him look older than his thirty-five years.

"Can I repay you?" I ask, teasing. His eyes rest on the tux hanging on the closet door. Clumsy with bandage, I unbuckle his belt. His eyes slide away from the tux.

"Sure. I'll take it out in trade," he says, helping me with his belt.

The show's over. Tom laces the back door flap shut. Under the horse tent, Tattoo Lou brushes her animals. Her assistant polishes the silver. He hangs the clean tack off the lines I never replaced. A wasted afternoon. When I pass the stakeline, I check for pulled stakes. All the guylines are secure, but I wish they weren't, so I could drive more stakes. Then I realize I couldn't swing a sledge with my gimpy hand. I kick the steel stairs on my way in the sleeper. They clang once in protest. Halfway in, I decide I need to walk. I slam the door shut. I don't care where I go; just away from the lot, away from town.

The wind lifts my hair off my neck, and I think about shaving it off. My muscles tighten and relax with each step, and I imagine getting fat; protective yellow globs coating my internal organs, shielding me. Sun on my skin, I think about burning it off and leaving shiny tight scars, like Tante's. I jump over the security fence and pick up the pace. Imagine growing in my armpit hair, my leg hair, and getting so strong my body looks more like a man's than a woman's. Cutting off my breasts, sewing myself shut. I think about my child's body under Pa's and wonder what I advertised then, with my hairless flat self.

Running now, running. I think about Pa, the nailhead, falling, falling out. How I called Pa's penis "him" as if it had its own brain. How else could Pa be so different, with two different halves of himself? Out of breath, I slow to a walk. My pinkie throbs with my slowing heart.

I turn around and walk back to the show. I concentrate on my breath, my heart. I collapse inwards. Focus on milkweed seeds blowing past my eyes. A meaningless pattern of white. Something to get lost in.

At home, I stand on Al's bunk to reach the top of the wall unit, where he stores his precious Cabernet Sauvignon. He calls it "Cab Salve." There are three bottles. Enough for me. Tomorrow I'll go back to town to replace them.

May
1985

▲

Falling

▲

Dairy farms, set in a shallow green valley rimmed with mountains; one ash-colored road and two blocks of buildings. This is Abundance. I tie the last knot on the last rain-cap just as the sun clears the charcoal peaks. For a few moments, the white bigtop turns gold beneath my bare feet. Then the sky becomes an overturned bowl, cloudless, blue like five-and-dime eye shadow or cornflowers. The smell of silage, corn and hay mush fermenting in silos, sweetens the air. Black and white cows munch grass, everywhere but town and the circus lot.

Driving in, I passed a white sign lit up from underneath, so as to be read easy at night: "Welcome to Abundance: Taste the freshness of our dairy!" Someone had spray-painted "air" after the word "dairy."

We set up in the 4-H County Fairgrounds, just south of the two blocks called Main Street. Main Street and town are one and the same. A grange hall, a grocery, three brands of Christianity housed in three white buildings—shingle, aluminum siding, and stucco—a flat brick ugly school, a library, a hardware, and a bar. At the fairgrounds, Main turns back into County Route 416. The fairgrounds are a big field, big dirt parking lot, and temporary-looking hangars made from corrugated plastic. Tom says these are for housing the animal husbandry and home canning displays. A slat board and wire snow fence surrounds the grounds, but we've set up our yellow security fence anyhow, inside it. Drawing a tighter circle around our trailers and trucks and tents.

The lot is post-move empty, the crew finally sleeping after three days of catnaps. We had two shows last Sunday, loaded out till just before dawn, drove all Monday, and set up till this morning, Tuesday. There's a show this afternoon at four; another this evening. We joke that Sunday, Monday, and Tuesday only exist in the real world outside our yellow security fence. In the circus calendar it is all one day: Moveday.

On the ground again, feet cold from the early morning dew, I lift my elbow towards the sky and test-sniff my armpit. I hope the water's been hooked up to the shower truck. I'm filthy and rank. From three days of no washing, no sleep, heavy labor, too much truck stop coffee, and too many cigarettes. So all I'm thinking is get a hot shower before the rest of the crew wake up.

I open the carnival painted door to the showers. An unfamiliar voice screams, "Shut the door, you're letting all the cold air in!"

I stand frozen on the shower truck steps, knob in hand, door open wide. A huge woman takes up most of the tiny room. No, maybe not quite a woman; she looks closer to my age, maybe slightly older, early twenties at the most. I can't help but stare; first off, she's someone I've never seen before; secondly, she's naked; and lastly, she's very pregnant.

"You new here?" I ask, though I know she is, of course.

"Just got off the bus."

"From?"

"Sarasota." Milky mirrors line the wall behind the sinks. Her tiny nose close to the glass, she stares at herself. She inspects her face for something. Pimples? Stray hairs?

"Oh . . . " My voice trails off, and I'm not sure what to say next. I make a show of unpacking my soap and shampoo into a shower stall, as if to prove I'm just here to take a shower, not to pry. Slowly I shuck my clothes, carefully folding them on the only dry spot on the Formica sink bank. I wait for her to say something. She doesn't seem interested in me at all. She's plucking her eyebrows, though the faint blond arches look perfect to me. Not at all like the dark caterpillars marching across my browbones. I wish I'd paid more attention when Al tried to show me how to shape my brows.

"You know"—I lean casually against the warped wood paneling—"some summers ago we all joked that we were gunning for the record of the most pregnant women on one lot in circus history." I clutch the towel to my flat belly with my elbows. It feels rough against my skin. I tick the names off on my fingers. "We had Tom's first wife—Darlene; Jacomo's wife; Fabrizio's wife—he's the ringmaster, she just sells concessions; high-wire Giselle—her husband hadn't left yet—and elephant Sadie. But they left after their elephant squished a roustabout against a truck, so we never got to see the baby."

All these wives sat around in lawn chairs, rubbing cocoa butter into stretched out skin as their bellies ripened in the sun, looking like watermelons ready to burst from their own internal pressure.

"Mmm," she hums to the mirror. Her belly rests in the bowl of a faucetless sink. Of the three sinks, only the one in front of me still has all its hardware.

"When are you due?" I ask. Maybe we'll become friends and she'll let me hold the baby.

"Within the month, but I hear firsts are usually late," she says.

"This your first?" I ask.

"Yeah."

That summer, the summer of all those pregnant women, I could barely wait to hold the babies. But when they were born, the mothers kept their babies close. My hands were always too dirty, or they were nursing, or crying. I asked Giselle how it felt to hold a baby, and she said it's the best thing in the world, better than falling in love. This pregnant girl has the same glow in her eyes. My calluses and nails are black with Moveday dirt, so I hide my hands behind my back, and my towel drops to the puddled tiles.

Embarrassed, I rewrap my towel around my small breasts. It's damp from the floor, but I'd rather be wet than naked. I say, "You married?"

She speaks to her reflection. "No, but I'm gonna be, once Jay finds out about his new little guy."

Jayson. I run dirty fingers over my cracked lips. She holds my gaze in the mirror, and I feel filthier than before. The pregnant girl lapses into silence, concentrating on the pink plastic curlers she rolls into limp blond hair.

I lean over the cream counter and stare into my large pores. My sharp nose, crooked from breaks, my ragged tangled hair, dark with dust and grease. Her nose is tiny, turned up at the tip, dotted with freckles. She looks out of place in this foul narrow room, and I feel too much like a natural part of it. Black mildew fur grows in the cracked Formica. The piss yellow tiles under my bare feet feel soft, like a rotten bleacher board. The shower curtains smell poisonous, like the inside of a new truck on a hot day. Black hair spirals cling to the greenish drains, the blistered white walls. I can't catch my breath.

A shower isn't so important right now.

"Suddenly I'm real tired," I mutter.

"Mmm." She nods. She doesn't look at me.

I pull my salty sweatshirt back over my head; drop my towel on the wet tiles. My jeans catch going over my naked hips; I stuff crunchy underwear in my back pocket.

"Maybe I should sleep now, shower later." She waves me off with a thin smile and a flick of her wrist, then goes back to tracing her lips with a red pencil. I back out the shower truck, trying to ignore the lump of ice that has settled into my guts, while she grins at herself in the fogged-up mirror, stroking her white mound soft and slow.

Empty card tables and folding chairs crowd the cookhouse tent. Behind the aluminum prep station, Al mixes Spam chunks into elbow macaronis with fluttery hands, mumbling about not getting any work done around here with all the disturbance. Eleven already, lunch in an hour, how will he ever finish?

Sun streams through the cookhouse tent walls, glints off its aluminum frame. The once clear vinyl walls are filmy from use, the silver frame graying and scratched. I tip back in my steel fold-out chair and take a long drink from his Jim Beam.

"Lordy-loo, will you please use a glass, you heathen." He shakes a Spam covered finger at me.

"You don't," I say.

"Exactly, so I don't want to catch anything from you."

"Hey now," I say, "I have half a mind to be insulted."

Al wrinkles his nose. "You do smell nasty, Girlfriend."

"Now I am insulted." Al waves a dish towel at me, as if clearing the air.

"It's been Moveday. Give me a break. Listen, I'll chop onions, if you'll give up a little cheezma." I'm surprised at how casual I sound.

"Oh, now Miss Thing wants information along with my cocktails." He snatches his bottle back. "Anything else I can get you, dearie? A canapé? A cigarette?"

"Don't mind if I do." I shake a Virginia Slim out the box on the table. Al throws the back of his hand to his forehead in a gesture of futility and frustration. He sighs.

I point my chin towards the onions. He snatches three out the overhead basket and juggles them a few times round. Years ago, Al was a clown; this was his old routine. Costumed in a flowered housedress, exaggerated eye-lashes, puckered lips, a blond wig, he played a harried housewife-clown, juggling groceries, rubber babies, laundry, diapers, produce. Three clockwise circles, a few over-hand arches. He rolls them across his forehead. Onions balance on his chin, ear, the bridge of his nose. Then pop off his light brown elbow, one at a time. Perfect aim; each bulb heads straight for my heart. I catch all but one, which I have to chase around the kitchen floor before it stops at his feet.

"Getting a bit slow, girlie." He hands me a cutting board, and I grab a long knife from the rack.

"Yeah, well, I've got more than onions on my mind." I take my board to the table.

"I suppose we met Kelli." Al wipes the Spam off on his gingham apron and sits across from me, his slim brown fingers warming around a cup of coffee. "Kelli with an *i,*" he says.

I ignore him. After a bit of chopping, I say, "Are you hinting that shithead is with her?" My words squeeze, thin and hard, around the cigarette clenched between my lips.

"Ooh, I do believe Miss Thing is jealous. Give up on that sorry-man Jayson." He tastes his coffee, then adds a shot of Beam. "I swear you'd be better off if you just found yourself a nice girlfriend. Men are bitches, all of them. They always want more, more, more."

Another burning shot of Beam. I ask, quietly now, "What the hell kind of name is Kelli with an *i?*" The knife frozen, midair, gut level. I stab it into the cutting board. "Kelli." It hits the roof of my mouth hard, then settles soft and rotten on my tongue, like moldy bread.

"Kelli," Al says, "is the kind of name little white ladies give their little white girls so they can spell their little name with little hearts over the *i.*"

"What's the *i* for, Al?"

He tilts his cup and throws his coffee to the back of his throat. He shudders once, then says, "*I* is for . . . I think she gonna steal your man." His voice is steady, quiet. He's serious, I realize.

"When did this happen?" I stub my butt out on the heel of my clogs and flick the filter out the door.

He leans forward in his chair, lowers his voice. "Well, now I heard this all from Tante, so it's secondhand, but she swears on the Virgin that it happened when they were rehearsing on her property, so I got to believe her."

Above the grill, flies die on the yellow glue strip. My stomach sinks; an achy hollow space burns in its place.

"Yeah, and so?" I begin more onions, careful to arrange my face blankly. I concentrate on the smell of onions, their slippery skin. My onion stained fingers bring tears to my eyes, but I don't blink and let the tears spill over.

"Well, Kelli was a showgirl on Great Southwest. Web act. So they all were wintering down near Sarasota, right near Tante's spread. And who went down to Tante's to deliver costumes last winter quarters?" His voice drawls upwards with a you-fill-in-the-blank note.

"Jayson." My dirty hands leave black shadows on the clean white onions.

"Yes, Girlfriend!" He snaps his long fingers and shrieks.

I take more of his booze. I pour another shot for him.

"Yeah, and so?"

"So this winter he did more than deliver costumes. While we all were freezing our ta-tas at winter quarters in Rhinekill, Mr. Jayson sat Miss Kelli's web, if you get my drift."

The web is an act for no-brainers, no talent. Usually it's just a rope with a hand loop three-quarters the way up. Then it's rigged to spin freely from the top of the tent. The showgirl climbs up, aided by the sitter. He pulls and releases the bottom of the rope while she wraps and unwraps her leg around it. This tension and release eases her up the rope, like those toy monkeys suspended from two strings. When a kid pulls on the strings, the monkey ascends because of friction. Tom explained this once, how it's pretty much the same with web girls.

When the showgirl reaches the top, she poses, then sticks her hand, or foot, or some other body part, in the loop, pulls down the safety, and the sitter starts swinging the rope around. Looks scary, but the biggest danger is puking. The web by itself is such a dull act that only mud-shows rely on it. Fabrizio only allows web work for mounting the wire or trapeze. No real danger, no net. The whole point of web is so guys below can check out the showgirl's butt. At least that's what I've heard from ringcrew. I can see where Al's story is leading.

He tips forward in his chair and covers his whisper with the back of his hand. But the smell of bourbon still drifts through his fingers.

"Seems like while our hero hung on that web, looking up at Miss Tramp wrapping her bony legs round and round that thick rope, he got ideas. She come sliding down and wrapped her legs round something else. Could you die?"

"I could die." I mean this differently than Al. The onions sit in innocent white piles, waiting to fry.

"Can you say, 'No pride'?"

I don't know who he's referring to now. "No pride," I echo. I light myself a Lucky; Al's Slims are too weak for me now.

Outside the cookhouse, a few circus kids run across the front lot, their laughter high pitched squeals. Jacomo's kids, Nunzio leading little Rozario, and the little Fabrizio, Petra. High wire Giselle's beautiful four-year-old daughter, Astrid, is It. They rush at her, then run away. She turns to touch them, and they screech through open laughing mouths. Giselle, her matinee costume protected from dirt by a terry-cloth robe, looks on, satisfied. She sits on the production trailer stairs, smiling at her daughter.

Giselle's body bounced back from pregnancy well; she was performing the next season, as graceful as ever. She never seemed upset that her man ran off. He never even met the baby. I'd trade places with her any day.

Al's voice pulls me back inside the cookhouse ". . . this no-pride, huntin' a man, leotard sportin', easy talkin', web-humpin', cheap young thing comes twitchin' her tail, sniffin' around—may I say—your man. And you know how lonely things get out there in the middle of nowhere. Next thing she know, she on her back with her legs in the air, shrieking, 'Jayson—Jayson—Jayson—give it to me!'" He grips the back of his chair and flings his feet on the table, legs spread wide. I move the onions out from under his descending slippers just in time.

Al sashays back to his cooking station. "Well, it's just not a party girl's world anymore. 'Cause you know that little tramp got herself pregnant." He scatters cubes of Spam across the noodle bed.

My head feels stuffed with words. I hand Al the onions and say, "They're all chopped." Tiny opal squares, like a child's fingernails, crowd the cutting board. "I hope that's how you wanted them."

"Thanks, Sugar." He grabs my face with his left hand and shakes his right forefinger in my eyes, like he's about to scold me. His fingers smell like meat.

"My poor Honey-bunny. He's just not worth it. Men are bitches; they all are." Now he holds me by my shoulders at an arm's length. "Listen. I'll see you back at the sleeper and we'll drink cocktails. You'll feel better after a few juleps."

"I'm fine, Al. Just fine," I say, backing down the cookhouse steps. Wave casually, just to show how fine I am.

Giselle calls to me, "Watch the kids tonight?" I think she said, "Want the kids tonight?" and I say yes, then realize I'm just being asked to baby-sit.

"Good. Seven o'clock," she says. I nod, make the thumbs-up sign. Giselle smiles at me from her perch on the stairs. She smiles at her daughter, Astrid, who just tagged Nunzio.

Nunzio is It now. The children surge forward, surrounding him, then whirl away when he turns towards them.

When I was a child, I played this game. I wonder when I

stopped playing. I remember the feverish, frightening excitement of tag. Will I be touched, will I touch? Wanting it, avoiding it, teasing. It reminds me now of sex, of Jayson. My stomach rolls over, and I walk quickly around the tent, hiding my face towards the bigtop sidewall.

I lean into the curve of blue. Clogs scuffle drying grass. My fingertips brush hot vinyl coated canvas, bump over sidepoles at every fifth step; my eyes blur the regular pattern of stars and stripes sewn into the sidewall. I count 54 poles, nearly halfway round the bigtop. Blinded by the sidewall pattern, I walk smack into Jayson. His arms fold around me, trapping me. I can't see his face, he holds me so close to his pocket tee. Three showerless days have sharpened his warm earthy smell to the metallic odor of just welded steel.

"Hey, Baby," he whispers, kissing my scalp. His Moveday stubble scratches my forehead.

I freeze. Not stiff, not limp, simply motionless and breathless until I can think what I want to do, to say.

He recognizes this tactic. "You're mad at me, aren't you?"

I still can't come up with a reply, so I don't move.

"Come on, Baby, let's go talk, Sugar." Arm soft around the back of my neck, he leads me to the tent truck and sets me in the shotgun seat. Then he walks round and gets behind the driver's side. A bumper sticker on the dashboard reads: "Hannibal the Cannibal says: Tattoos Taste Great! BodyART exotic Pierces and Tattoos—you got it, we'll stick a needle in it!" Saint Christopher and Saint Jude dangle from the rearview on graying chains. The windshield's splattered with bugs. We gaze quietly at the backlot as if we're going somewhere, instead of sitting still in a motionless truck. We stare at the generator, the flatbeds, the forklift. The piles of hay outside Tattoo Lou's horse tent. Jaq, the husband half of the Fabulous Farouks, sets a bright red body board against the hay bales. His wife, Luz, fits her small body into the white silhouette painted on the wood plank.

Jayson rests his hands on the wheel. It's covered with yellowing sheep wool. The seats are covered by woven wood bead mats, designed to massage our backs while driving long distances, but the beads press my skin in uncomfortable places. I wish I'd slept more, showered. I don't feel up to a fight.

Jayson looks over at me. "You gonna talk, Mat?"

With an onion thumb, I pick at a peeling corner of the bumper sticker on the dashboard.

"Talk to me, Babe." Jayson nuzzles my neck. "I can't kiss it better if you don't tell me what hurts."

Jaq Farouk tosses a long silver knife in the air. It flips three times, then lands neatly, handle first, in his waiting palm. He pulls two more from his waistband and juggles. The knives flash brilliantly in the early-morning sun. Jayson kisses my earlobe. Something warm drops from my womb and moistens my underpants.

I push him away. "She's pregnant. She's fucking out to here with your kid." My hands carve a space the size of a watermelon in front of my shirt.

"Hey now, how do you know that's my kid? Could be anybody's." He grabs my shaking hands out of the air and holds them quiet in his lap. "She tell you? Don't believe everything you hear, Mat."

I try to pull my hands out of his, but he grips my wrists tightly. "Did you sleep with her? Did you?" His eyes show nothing. "Wait," I say before he can answer. "I don't want to know. Don't tell me anything."

Jaq lets the knives fly. *Thwap—thwap—thwap.*

Jayson releases my hands. The knives quiver around Luz's head. One at each ear, and one directly above the straight white part in the exact center of her black hair. I slip out the door.

Walking back to my sleeper, I take a detour through the backlot. There's an unfamiliar red pickup with a shredding fiberglass camper cab attachment. Tante always says, "Know your enemy." So I leave a note stuck in the handle of the camper door: "Kelli wellcom to the lot lets take the kids to the show tonite. Meet you hear at 7.—Matilda from the showers." I know my spelling stinks, but she probably won't notice. She can't be any kind of brain surgeon if she got herself messed up with Jayson. Then I worry she can't read at all and maybe she won't understand the note. Finally I tell myself to stop worrying, not waste time on this. I just need to shower, to rest.

Halfway to my sleeper, I head back to the truck, take the note out the handle, and put a heart over the *i.* Then stuff it back in the handle. For the first time in days, I relax.

Kelli and me sit in the back row, separated by four small bodies: Jacomo's kids, Nunzio and Rozario; Petra Fabrizio; and Astrid, Giselle's kid.

The tent is hot already, and the band has just begun the overture. The kids' bodies give off a smell like overripe fruit, and the vinyl coated sidewall smells like last week's cotton candy. I feel vaguely ill and consider sliding down between the floorboards to the cool gray under-bleachers and watching the show through a garden of ankles. Maybe I would find Kelli's ankles, puffy with water retention, and pop the bloated flesh with my marlinespike.

In front of us, the audience settles down. Families in neat units crowd the bleachers. Blocky fathers, square shoulders in clean flannel plaids and overwashed chinos; soft, droopy mothers wearing hand crocheted cardigans over floral-print cotton shifts. Fat dairy-fed children, blond hair shiny with sunstreaks. The children next to me look wiry and foreign by comparison.

The little Italians scream, "Daddy! Daddy!" In their bouncing excitement they shake the bleacher bench. Kelli looks at me over their heads and beams; probably thinking about that lump in her stomach screaming Daddy at Jayson. I wonder: Why am I here? Shut up. I hit myself in the thigh with my clenched fist, hard. Watch the show.

Ringmaster Fabrizio kicks clown Jacomo through the bandstand curtain. Covered by their fake fight, Jayson directs his ringcrew boys in setting up Giselle's wire. The band blasts through a few jazzy chords of "More Than a Woman," and the rig is in place. Giselle steps through the gold velour curtain wearing hot pink sequins and feathers. Jayson, handsome in his tux, steps into the ring, a gallant, gracious gentleman. I could fall in love with him again, each time he wears that tux.

He accepts Giselle's sparkly cape, kneels to receive her high-heeled clogs, and backs off, bowing slightly. She is beautiful in her pink sequined bikini. Now it is Astrid's turn to scream, "Mommy." Both she and Kelli smile. And I shred the insides of my cheeks with my eyeteeth.

Giselle slowly climbs the web that Jayson steadies for her. She pauses briefly midway, to style in an arabesque and acknowledge her audience. Fabrizio stands off to the side in his red jodhpurs, black tails, and top hat, his handlebar mustache, styling with broad gestures in her direction. As if the audience needs his help deciding where to look.

We are riveted on Giselle, gracefully mounting the wire. She works without a net, though the act deserves one. Still, I hear the mother in front of us tell her child, "It's only meant to look dangerous, dear, just like the movies."

After a few expert passes, poses, Giselle rides across the wire on a bicycle, then a unicycle. Both grooved in the wheel to accommodate the thin steel cable.

Astrid gazes up at Kelli. "Mommy's teaching me. I could do that soon."

Giselle's final trick. She slides two leather hand tubes to the center of the wire, then handstands, gripping them. Her toes point straight to the cupola; her focus is steady, straight down to the ringdirt 50 feet below. She hovers, like a fancy trick diver frozen midair. The audience becomes quiet. Fists freeze inside popcorn bags. She tilts her pelvis, sending her body out of balance; the audience collectively gasps. Her body swings down, around, under the wire, and back up into a handstand, where she hovers suspended again. She rotates easily around the steel wire because the smooth leather tubes gripped in her hands defy the wire's friction. Having shown us the trick in slow-mo, Giselle begins the blow-off. She shifts her weight again, swings around the wire, no longer stopping at the top in a pose. Picking up speed with each rotation, spinning faster and faster, using her strong legs to propel her rotations. Mark keeps a white spot on her the whole time. Jayson stands below, chest expanding to fill his black tux, hands clasped behind his rigid back, eyes on Giselle's every move. If she falls, it is his job to break her impact with his body. The audience counts, prompted by Jacomo and Fabrizio.

"Nine! . . . Ten! . . . E-le-ven! . . . " I imagine spinning up, down, and around, hair streaming back from my face, wind blowing the knots out of my tired brain. The drummer hits his snare and bass with each completed spin. The beats come faster now. At twenty, Mark will black the spot for the briefest moment, and Jayson will run forward with the web. When the spot comes back, to the audience's horror, Giselle will have disappeared. But then Mark will pick her up in a light pink bubble of light, clinging safely to the web, securely steadied by Jayson's strong hands. Though I know this is how the trick ends, I ride along with the audience anticipation. I grab Astrid's hot small hand and squeeze it in my big icy one. We grin at each other and hunch our shoulders, like sisters in on a secret.

"Nineteen! . . . Twenty!" The spotlight blinks out, the last drumbeat hangs echoing in the dark tent. The audience holds its collective breath, then releases a sigh. A pink spotlight picks up the web. For a moment I also feel the expected relief. But the web hangs empty. Mark, unsure now, swings his spotlight down the web; he must have fixed it too high. The circle of pink light searches its length. The audience, still unaware, waits happily in the dark for the next delight. Astrid squeezes my hand so hard it hurts, but I notice with only half a mind. The web sways lightly, unsteadied by Jayson.

Then the pink spot picks them up in the ringdirt, just a snapshot. Jayson bent over Giselle. She is twisted like a forgotten toy, the sawdust around them spreading red.

Astrid screams, "Mommy!" Mark blacks the light. One heartbeat of fear, then a gear shifts in my brain. My mind erases the picture, and calm takes its place. This is not a time to feel or think. Time to act. My eyes focus sharply, clicking off possible escape routes. My hearing dissects sounds: Fabrizio shouting, the shuffle of ringcrew sneakers through sawdust, the brush of the curtain parting, sweeping closed, jangle of de-rigging, whispered conversations getting louder.

The band strikes up a Souza march, and the lights find Jacomo dancing around the hippodrome track, teasing the audience with his crazy antics. Fabrizio pretends to be annoyed by his clowning.

Kelli and I meet eyes over the kids' heads. "Let's get out of here," she says.

Our exit is crowded with panicked audience members, who are not fooled by the clown and the ringmaster. Bleacher boys in purple usher jackets block the exits, politely suggesting that all is fine, return to your seats. Round-eyed mothers grip their children by elbows and wrists, fathers bump shoulders and argue with each other, the crew, their wives. Ushers hold white gloved hands chest high, herding these townies back to their seats. Concessionaires join the crowd, distracting frightened children with silver balloons and rainbow sno-cones.

We can't get past the bodies. "Through here," I say, sliding between the floorboards, past the garbage nets to below the bleachers. I reach my hands up through the blue painted ply boards and catch the children Kelli hands down to me. We stand under green nylon hammocks filled with half-eaten hotdogs, wax paper cups, and sticky cotton candy cones. Feet stamp loudly overhead. I am proud of the children for waiting so quietly while Kelli maneuvers her girth above. Finally she removes a floorboard and climbs down the bleacher risers with surprising grace. We lift up the sidewall and shoo the children under and into the dark backlot.

The backlot is strangely silent after the confusion under the bigtop. The only lights shine from trailer windows on performer row, half hidden behind the curve of the bigtop. All around us, trucks squat, black and misshapen. Elephants sway behind us, their slow, steady rocking a rhythmic swish. Warm sweet smells rise from the dumpsters. I listen to my breath slow, my heart thump less. Adrenaline drains from my veins. A cool breeze slaps my face, and the last shred of calm disappears. Now my skin twitches and my mouth dries.

Kelli and I gather the children together, holding their little hands, sticky wet from crying. Kelli murmurs, "It's okay. Everything is okay. There's nothing to cry about. Everything is fine." Astrid's "Mommy, Mommy" fades into a quiet steady bleat. The others snuffle, no longer crying. After all, they saw their daddies performing on the hippodrome track and know their mommies are safely selling programs in the entrance chutes.

Kelli pulls Astrid away from the group and lies to her in a soft mother voice. An old piece of me buried somewhere between my lungs and stomach wakes up and burns. It wants Kelli to smooth my goose bumps and croon motherlike to me. I'm just as scared, I want to tell her.

The other children crowd around my knees, looking up in my face, waiting. They stare at me as if my big body makes me wise. I'd like to tell them: Hey, I'm as baffled as you. I avoid their wet eyes; instead I gaze at the clear sky filled with so many stars.

"When I'm scared," I tell them, "I look at things. If I look carefully enough, I forget to be scared. Look at the stars. There are so many." Obediently, they look up. "You know," I continue, "you can make wishes on stars. They're magic. Let's make a wish."

"For what?" asks Rozario.

"For Giselle to be okay, stupid," says Nunzio.

"I'm not stupid. You are!" Rozario leans her head against my hip. My hand finds her soft hair, and my fingers pull gently through her dark curls.

I say, "Let's not fight. Let's make wishes instead." Rozario sticks her wrinkled fingers in her mouth.

"Wishes don't work," says Petra, the oldest, always showing off.

"Do too," says Nunzio, looking for a fight with anyone.

"Do not," says Petra. "Tante says you have to pray to God in heaven if you want something."

Rozario removes her fingers. "Where's heaven?"

Petra points overhead. "Up there."

"So what's the difference?" Nunzio sticks his tongue out.

Petra crosses her arms. "There's a difference is all."

"Tell her." Nunzio tugs at my shirt.

"I don't know anything about heaven," I say. The trailers and mobile homes of their parents wait empty for the show to end. Behind them, the yellow security fence keeps us safe. Beyond that, dark silos in black pastures. My vision fails.

"Giselle's going to heaven," Petra says, so sure. She kicks a water hose dribbling in the dust.

"Why?" Rozario asks, but no one answers. We stand there looking at the stars scattered like seeds, listening to bugs and frogs scraping and croaking louder than the band.

An ambulance wails towards us and calls us back down from the sky.

"Let's get them out of here," Kelli says. She knows what to do. I wonder if her motherly instinct has grown with her belly. She takes the hands of Nunzio and Rozario; Petra follows behind. I take Astrid's damp palm in my own cold fist, and we run to the red pickup with the camper cab attachment.

"You'll make a good mother," I say. For some reason I don't understand, I feel the need to pay this woman a compliment. Some part of me wishes things were different, that she could be my friend. My sister. My mother.

The children sleep fitfully across her camper bed, curled into each other like a litter of puppies huddling for warmth. They are quiet; for a few hours they will forget what they saw. As soon as we'd reached her door, Kelli pulled down a bottle of Beam and poured six bourbon and gingers, forcing one down each child's throat till they passed out in her kitchenette. Now she and I sit finishing the bottle.

"Yeah, I know to get a child to sleep in an emergency." Kelli laughs and sips from her glass. "I really shouldn't have this." She holds up the drink and gazes at her stomach.

"Yeah, well, there's a lot of things we shouldn't do. Cheers." I finish my glass and pour more. The warm liquor spreads through my chest like a comforting blanket. I can handle Kelli, I think. It will be okay, I tell myself. The liquor glows in my stomach, and I know there's a way to fix this mess. The ambulance siren recedes.

"What do you suppose Jayson's doing?" I wonder out loud. My voice sounds surprisingly thick.

"Probably crowd control." She smiles at me and pats my hand across the table. "That was pretty bad," she says. "I'm glad we were together."

She doesn't know. I realize Kelli doesn't know. He hasn't told her about me. He hasn't said, "Hey, there's this woman I fuck every so often. We don't live together, but we fuck every so often for the past four years. Since she turned 15. Everyone knows."

Her blurry gaze holds no suspicion. She's probably thinking of him right now. Imagining her man telling the panicked crowd, "It's going to be all right. Everything is going to be just fine. If you'll please step back into the tent, we will continue the show."

Kelli finally speaks. "Poor Giselle. I'm sure she won't work after this." She doesn't say, "if she survives." "Poor Astrid." She gazes at the kids.

Someone should tell this woman what's up. How can she sit there rubbing her belly like an absentminded cow, feeling sorry for Giselle? I pour myself another. What about her? When is someone gonna tell her? Shit.

"There really isn't much for her to do here if she can't perform. I suppose she could sell tickets. You know, even if she's really hurt. That's a sit-down job. But with that salary, she won't be able to keep her trailer. I can't imagine living in a sleeper with a kid."

Suddenly I want to slap her. I want to shake her, yell, "Wake up! Don't you know who I am? Stop being so nice, dammit."

Instead I explain, "Tom won't allow it. Only performers and crew chiefs get trailers; no kids in sleepers. She's fucked."

I unroll my Luckies from my sleeve. Kelli leans back in her chair and snags an ashtray off the green kitchenette counter. It's a fake pink scallop shell, rimmed in gold paint. "Florida, the Sunshine State," in turquoise script, peeks out under old ashes and lipstick stained filters.

"Tom's letting me keep this pickup here till I get settled in with Jayson."

"Whatever," I mumble.

Kelli reaches for my pack, and I let her take a cigarette. "This same thing happened to a gal on Great Southwest; it was so tragic. I mean, not exactly the same thing, but close. She didn't fall or anything, but her man left her and their two kids, and she didn't have anything to fall back on." She helps herself to my lighter. After a long drag, she continues.

"He broke up the act by leaving with this other chick to work Circus-Circus in Vegas. And so there she was without the dogs—they had this dog act—and without the talent to start a new act. He was the trainer; she just stood there handing him stuff. You know, the hoops and balls and shit. He took all that when he took the dogs."

Blue-gray smoke curls from her frosty lips while she speaks, settles in the cheap poly curtains. They match the kitchenette cushions, large green roses splashed across cream stripes on a mustard background. I trace the roses next to my thighs, pick pills from the slippery fabric, and throw them on the dingy gold carpet.

I swig from the bottle and clear my throat. Her voice becomes background noise; I squeeze my soggy brain for what to say. She rambles on, and I have nothing to do with my mouth and hands but smoke and drink.

"Anyways, she finally gets this job selling programs, but it was so tragic. The kids ran around like animals; she didn't have time to take care of them because she had to do all these extra jobs to keep up her truck and trailer payments . . . " Blah, blah, blah. She's covering her mouth, giggling. I close my right eye and bring the room back in focus.

Her cigarette has burned down in the ashtray, ignored after the first puff. She grinds it out and titters a bit behind tiny fingers. "You know, smoke makes me so nauseous now, but I just can't quit. Old habit. You know?"

"Yeah. I know." This is pathetic; this is fucking pathetic. Don't you know? I have to tell her. In a couple more minutes I'll tell her. I just need another shot before I tell her. The fluorescent minute hand on her stove clock points to a glowing 5. When it hits the 6 I'll set her straight.

A moment of gray and my cigarette is finished. I'm lighting another. The minute hand's on the 8, but I was watching it and I never saw it move. My head is all loose on my neck and won't stay in one place. I rest it against the cool bug screen on the open window next to me. A breeze brushes the ugly curtains against my nose. They smell like bacon.

She's saying, "I don't know what I would do if I were Giselle. . . . We should take up a collection or something. I mean—"

"Jayson is with me," I say.

"—she must have expenses."

"Jayson is with me," I repeat.

She fixes her cow eyes on me. I watch a glimmer of recognition creep into her flaccid cow face. The muscles in her slack cheeks tighten; now her brain is working. I can practically see the gears crank. I almost laugh at the vision of gears turning in a mechanical cow head, but suddenly I can't remember why that was funny two moments ago.

And then somehow we are standing, stooped over, heads touching the low ceiling. I'm losing time here; moments slip past unrecorded. I shake my head to clear it, but all I hear is a rush of blood in my ears. I watch her mouth working, and words float towards me, meaningless sound.

Then the bottle is in my hand. A few inches left.

I look again; it's empty and my mouth burns.

I hear myself speak, thick and growly. "If your baby looks a thing like Jayson, you better watch it, 'cause I might just . . . " I lose the thread. Break it? Hurt it? Where did that come from?

The camper tilts; green Formica slides, melting into the mustard upholstery.

"Better not . . . " I begin my threat again. Better not . . . what? I wonder. I stand firm, legs wide to balance in the rocking room. My hand tightly grips the bottle neck. . . .

Now the bottle is shattered on the floor and the children are awake, crying.

"Get out of here!" she yells. Her blond pigtails loom at me. Her hand connects with my cheek, the limp slap of a weak woman. More like a caress. Jayson'll show her how to throw a punch.

Now I laugh. I laugh at her fat belly moving as she screams, I laugh at the ashes dirtying her manicured hand as she lets the ashtray fly. It breaks useless at my feet. I laugh and I can't hear what she says anymore. I back out the screen door, tumble down the steps. Walk away, laughing so hard tears fill my eyes and roll down my cheeks.

The lot is empty, show over, go home. I lean against a sidepole, loop my hand through the rope for support. Everyone needs a little support now and then, I think.

All the beautiful stars. Spinning, beautiful stars melting in salt water. The rope slips from my hand. There'll be a burn mark on my palm in the morning, I think. My head bounces. I smell the wet fertile scent of growing grass and realize I'm lying next to the back door of the tent. It'll be all right, I tell myself. It's okay. I'll just roll under the sidewall here, sleep in the tent. It's going to be all right. Everything is going to be just fine.

"You didn't come home last night, Sugar-booger." Al pouts behind a pile of biscuits and white cream gravy. "I had the cocktails all ready for a nice ladies' night, and you ditch me without even a by-your-leave."

The smell of frying eggs makes me want to puke.

"What with all the confusion," I start to explain, but then I think: Who gives a fuck? "Man, I have a full-on headache, Al. Don't give me any shit today, okay?" I go for the coffee. On second thought, I add sugar to get my blood going again.

"I see we are taking our coffee black and sweet. Too bad you don't take your men that way, Honey-bunny. Were you with that mean redneck last night? Is that why Miss Thing is so crotchety?" He purses his lips and shakes a finger. "And he a father, too."

I stick a Lucky between my lips. My mouth tastes like I've been licking bleacher boards. "Don't fuckin' start with me, Al."

"Ooh! Miss Thing is in a nasty temper." He lights my cigarette with a nickel-plated circus souvenir lighter. Then he snaps it shut with a quick wrist flick.

I ignore this comment, drink my coffee in peace. I sit in a steel folding chair, back turned against the morning sun. Soon the crew will be piling in here for breakfast.

"So," I say, "any news on Giselle?"

"Well, she's alive." He pulls a cardboard can of purple Kool-Aid from the cabinet.

"Yeah, and?"

He dumps half the powder into the bug juice jug and thumps the canister onto the service table, unnecessarily loud. Lavender dust floats up in a cloud around his hand.

"And there's the ever present and useless collection box à la Tante." He styles in the direction of a shoebox with the sign GISELLE written in purple crayon on the side.

"Yeah, and?"

"And what do you expect? By the time we get the real story, we'll be collecting for someone else!" He's dumping quarts of water into the jug with an old handleless saucepan. Water spashes over the sides, spots up the dusty floor. "And the kid'll go to some grandparents somewhere if there are any, and Fabrizio will line up a new act, and the show will go on."

Al finishes the juice and screws the red lid on the yellow jug.

"Yeah, well, whatever," is all I can think of to say.

"Yes. Brilliant; whatever!" Al shouts, his voice dropping deep in his chest. A bellow.

"Jesus, Al, I just said I got a fucking hangover; why you gotta yell? Fuck." I bang my fist on the table, and scalding coffee sloshes over my cup and onto my wrist.

For a moment, Al stares at me with the saucepan forgotten in his hand. Then he throws it in the sink, a painful clatter of aluminum landing in the steel basin.

"Oh yeah, I forgot Miss Thing. I was too busy worrying about Giselle to concentrate on your extreme pain. Can you ever forgive my thoughtlessness?" Sarcasm soaks his voice.

"Ah, fuck you," I mutter. My back crawls with an ugly feeling. I can't quite remember what I did last night.

Al reaches for a pitcher hanging over his head. "That's right, Mat." He throws it in the sink, and I cover my ears. "Fuck me"—he throws a ladle—"fuck you"—he slams a frying pan on the counter—"fuck everyone"—a dish breaks against the wall—"fuck everything!" He sweeps the dish drainer full of silverware onto the floor. "Let's get fucked." He grabs a bottle of vanilla extract and up-ends it into his mouth. "We're all fuck-ups. Life is fucked: fuck-*fuck*-FUCK!" Brown drops of saliva fly onto the eggs warming in the steam table.

I slap my hands on the table and kick my chair back with my knees. It clatters to the ground behind me, but I don't care; I give it another kick for good measure. "You know, Al, I could use a little support right now," I hiss through my gummy teeth. "I don't need your drama queen hysteria. It is not my problem Giselle is idiot enough to work without a net. Goddammit, there's no net every time I rig the fuckin' tent. There's never a fuckin' *net* for *me!*" My chest heaves, and I can't quite catch my breath.

We stare across the trashed cookhouse at each other. I could punch him. I could reach down his skinny neck and rip his heart out his prissy mouth. My fingers itch with the urge to strangle Al, then turn my hands on myself. This is not about Al, I say in my head. I count the flies on the glue strip and flex my toes against the hard wood soles of my clogs. I will not hit him, I tell myself over and over.

Al puts his back to me and whispers, "Did anyone ever tell you you're self-centered?"

"No, Al, who was gonna tell me? My ma?" I slam out the cookhouse door, my anger turned bitter, like the coffee grounds stuck in my teeth.

The damp grass darkens my clogs, but the sun is already hot, burning the field dry brown. I'm relieved to get out of the sun and into the cool blue shade under the canvas. The ringcrew rearranges props under the bandstand. The ring doesn't show any sign of Giselle's landing. Jayson comes through the gold velour curtain with a rake for the ringdirt. I can't deal with him right yet, so I escape up the mast. I don't look down to see if he sees me or not. I don't care.

When I emerge through the bale ring to the outside sky, the world is overbright with light reflected off the white canvas. Mirrored sunglasses out the pocket, onto the face. At least there's a breeze up here. The flags slap with a wind not felt on the ground.

The lot below is colorful with red concessions tents and blue banners. The confusion of trailers and mobile homes is just gray rectangles from this view. A line of yellow fence, a rusty storm fence, then fields and fields and cows and mountains and sky and sky and sky, and maybe if I stay up here long enough I'll dissolve and float away. I wish that.

Maybe Tom won't see me up here. Maybe he'll leave me alone long enough to work out this hangover. I should've eaten something. Always helps to have something in your belly. I would've if Al hadn't been such a bitch.

Below, people go about their morning duties. Elephants and horses are watered and fed, roustabouts mill around between the sleepers, the cookhouse, the shower truck. Lounging in lawn chairs, sharing a thermos of something steaming between them, Farouk polishes his knives and Luz files her nails. Further down performer row, Jacomo and Fabrizio, bathrobed, gripping coffee mugs, gesture at each other. The children play in grass-stained pajamas out front of their trailers. Somehow they got home all right; less to feel guilty about. I watch Tante cross the grass with her arms full of sequined leotards. She stops to talk to a concessions lady busy blowing up Mylar balloons. I wonder what they are talking about. Giselle's fall? Kelli and her baby? What a sucker I am? I tap a cigarette from my pack.

Maybe I should just go to another show. Maybe my time here is played out. I sit on top of the cupola, smoking, ticking off the possibilities in my mind. What other show would take a female on tent crew? Not graceful enough for showgirl, can't cook, no patience for tickets.

My cigarette burns down to my fingers, and I light another off it. I rub the cold ashes into my jeans; I store the spent butt in my pocket.

What to do about Al? I really messed that up. Where am I gonna sleep tonight? Al's pissed, and I can't go crawling to Jay's. I really need a rest. A break. If only there was a way to hold a moment still, long enough to figure things out. Life is moving just too fast, I think. By itself, taken alone without last night or tonight, this is a fine moment. If only I could hang on to it a bit longer, so I could make plans.

"Hey, Babe. Looking for company?" Jayson climbs up over the bale ring with a Styrofoam cup clenched between his teeth.

I can't take this right now, I think.

"Fuck off," I say.

"Hey now, I come up here with coffee for you, Babe, and that's what I get? Well, I guess I'll drink it myself." He sits next to me and takes a sip.

"Did you rake up all the blood, Jay?" I wonder if I could jump off the tent.

"I'm gonna pretend you didn't say that, Mat. You know that was just an accident," he says. "It's not my fault she works without a net."

With my luck, I'd probably just be crippled. I decide not to jump today.

"Shit," I say. I don't want to look at him. He slides nearer to me and kisses behind my ear.

"What's the matter, Baby? Why you so mean?" He traces the ash stain on my thigh with his thick index finger.

"I just had a fight with Al." That's not what I wanted to say, but it's what came out.

"That all, Baby? You two'll make up. That's nothing. You can stay with me till it blows over."

"Yeah, well, what about Kelli? Doesn't she sleep with you now?" I slap his circling hand off my leg.

"Hey now, hey . . . I'm sorry I didn't tell you. I never knew she was gonna show up here." He is giving me the sincere face. I can hear it in his voice, even though I don't look at him.

"Are you gonna let her move in with you? She says she's gonna. You know Tom won't let her keep her camper for too long. She thinks you're gonna marry her."

He takes my chin gently in his hand and turns me to face him. His dark, smooth skin hangs over solid cheekbones. Already, a stiff beard darkens his square jaw. Crepe paper skin wrinkles gently around his brown tired eyes. He strokes my rigid cheek with the back of his hand and says, "Shh, shh."

Clouds shadow the white canvas. The yellow and blue flags snap. I will myself to sit up straight. He puts his arm around me to pull me close. I will not lean into the crook of his armpit.

"Hey now, hey. Who am I with? Who do I love?" His lips brush these words into my temple. "That was one night; I was really drunk. I regret it; I'm really sorry. We had nothing together, and I was drunk that night."

"That's no excuse," I say. "I get drunk and you don't see me losing control like that." Wind plays across the cables supporting the cupola. Come-along cables thrum inside the masts. All four bale rings vibrate in sympathy. It's going to rain; there'll be no sleeping outside for me tonight.

"Listen, things are really hard for me right now, you know? I can't stand for us to be fighting. Giselle's accident, and this thing with crazy Kelli . . . " He sighs. "I don't want to lose you. We need to be together. We need to spend time together." His voice drops in pitch. "I'll come to your sleeper tonight, we can talk. We'll figure something out; we always do, right?"

I am so tired. I could lean on him just a little bit. I could maybe just lean on him a little. "It's not fair that you get to be nice now," I whisper into his neck.

"Shh, shh. We'll be together tonight. Who am I with? Shh." He rocks me back and forth, back and forth.

His weight is heavy on my stomach. I imagine having weight there all the time. He moves down to my breasts and licks the right one. I lift my head to watch his tongue tease my nipple erect. I watch him suck it, and wonder if he could draw milk from there. I remember Tante telling me about wet nurses in the old country; she said women could nurse whether they had been pregnant or not, that the milk was drawn to their breasts by the act of a baby sucking every two hours. I wonder, If Jayson sucked at my breasts every two hours, would the milk come?

He is moving on my hips; he is in me now. I grab him by the lower back and press him against my belly, enjoying his heaviness. I rub the swell of his arched back like Kelli rubs her stomach.

"I want to feel you come inside me."

He moves harder and faster.

"I want you to come deep inside me." I think of the diaphragm sitting in my top drawer.

"Come inside me, fill me up," I murmur. He stops moving.

"What is up with you?" He lifts his face off my shoulder and meets my eyes. He looks for a clue, but I don't give him any. I move my hips under him, push my hands against his butt to get him going again. His back is stiff, resisting. I turn my head to the pressboard wall, inspecting the fake wood grain for splinters, loose nails. I count to twenty. When I look back, he is still hovering there.

I feel him get soft. Eventually he falls out, and I am left disappointed and empty. He pulls back on his knees and stares at me.

"What is up with you?" he asks again, baffled. Growing angry.

"I want a baby." I want your baby is what I meant to say, and try to correct myself, but his hand comes down hard across my face before I get the chance to explain. We look at each other. I feel my cheek throb four, five times before I close my eyes.

As I roll away, his limp penis slides wet over my hip. My back to him, I curl up.

"Hey now, hey. I'm sorry." He strokes my hair.

I do not hear him. The light behind my eyelids glows red.

"You took me by surprise is all. I have enough problems already, you know? I'm sorry." His lips brush the top of my ear.

He is not there. I watch changing patterns of light and dark.

I feel the bunk shift as he stands up. I hear him find his pants, coins and rigging knife jingling as he pulls them on.

"I'm sorry," he says.

I wait a long time after the door slams before I move.

In the mirror my stomach is flat, my breasts are small and hard. I am empty; nothing is growing in there. No babies, no milk. I think. A woman can be defined by what is growing in her; Kelli by what is in her womb, and myself by what is not. She is a mother. I am not. She will be the mother of Jayson's child. Myself . . . I choose not to think on this.

Mother. The word weighs heavy in my mouth.

I turn away from the mirror and turn off the light. I wish Al was here. Probably sleeping in the cookhouse, curled up behind the steamers with a bottle for a teddy bear.

Half a step to my bunk. Under the covers, I curl my knees to my empty chest. I rock myself, thinking I won't fall asleep.

I close my eyes anyway. I dream Kelli and I are behind the tent. She reaches under her shirt and pulls out her baby. Her stomach grows flat, and I feel mine swelling as she hands her child to me. She says, If you want the man, you'll need the baby.

Yes, I say. I reach with outstretched hands, but she is too far away.

Jayson is there too. He says, Don't do this; you don't have to do this. He speaks to all of us.

I can almost reach the child, a little girl. With a swift slicing motion, Jayson knocks my arms down, and the baby falls to the cement. Her head opens like an overripe watermelon.

It's going to be all right, everything is going to be just fine; there is plenty here for everyone, I say, reaching down for a piece of the sugary fruit. Pink sugar-water pulp runs down my forearm when I lift it to flick a black seed off my elbow with my tongue. Black seed, green rind, and pink flesh cover the ground. Save the seeds, I tell Kelli, one secreted between my cheek and gum. We can plant another, I tell Jayson, as I touch that secret seed with my tongue.

July
1985

▲

The Canvas Boss

▲

There are two queen-sized beds in the room. The one on the left is nearer the bathroom, the one on the right nearer the door and the TV. Perhaps I should consider this, but I am too tired to think any further, so I drop my bag on the right-hand bed. I have driven over 20 hours to get to Sarasota in time to meet Tom at the airport. Now I can get a few hours' sleep before we have to pick up the concessions wagon, order the new entrance tent, and drive back.

Tom stands in the open doorway, looking out at the pool.

"Nice," he says.

"Yeah, that's why I chose this motel," I say.

"Good girl."

"Yeah, well . . . listen, I'm feeling real gross. I'm gonna change, okay?"

"Sure, don't mind me. We got a couple hours before we have to do business."

"Fine." In the bathroom I change into a pair of sweats

and a tee-shirt. I consider showering, but I'm too far gone. I figure I'll shower later, before we have to pick up the wagon and deal with the tent. I try to lock the bathroom door, but the little button in the handle won't stay pushed in. I finally give up. Tom knows I'm in here changing; he won't come in.

Tom has always treated me just like a daughter, though I'm not his kid or stepkid even. When I first started working, stuck in the costume truck, hating it, it got so I was ready to scream if I saw another torn pair of fishnets. I hung around the tent during tear-downs and set-ups just to get my hand in whenever I could. Just for a little excitement. Occasionally, Tom would teach me something. How to tie sidewall, how to splice a line. He even took me to the top of the tent and showed me how to lace. When my real stepdad, Pa, slid off the bigtop, a position opened up on tent crew. I already knew the ropes; Tom let me take Pa's spot. I've been ever grateful to him for rescuing me from wardrobe. And secretly pleased to be the first female roustabout he can remember hearing about. This business trip has been rough, but it is still far better than sewing tights.

When I come out the bathroom, Tom is lying on the left-hand bed with his boots on, smoking a Marlboro. I cross in front of him. "Tom, I'm way tired, so I'm gonna get some sleep, okay?"

"Sure," he says.

I lie down on the right-hand bed, nearer the TV. It's too hot for all the covers, so I sit up and fold them down to the edge and lie back again. But I don't like lying there with no cover at all, so I sit up again and pull just the sheet over me. I flop over on my right side and face the door.

"Jesus, Matty. You always like that? How does Jayson put up with all your fidgeting?"

"I don't stay over." Tom knows I don't stay over Jayson's anymore. Tom knows Jay lives and sleeps with Kelli now. He and Patsy double with them all the time. He knows Jay and me just fuck.

Jay and me were together before Kelli weaseled her way into his trailer. Kelli knew that and she decided to live with him anyhow. It's common knowledge that he and I are still together. He likes it with me, but he also likes living with her, for now. I always turn him down when he asks me to move in. I won't move in unless we're married. Kelli thinks because she says her baby is his, Jayson'll marry her. But he won't. I know. I know him better than anyone. Even though he says he feels some kind of obligation to her. Sometimes I feel sorry for Kelli because she's so blind to the truth. But I won't feel guilty when she leaves. She knew what she was getting into.

My thoughts blur towards sleep. Then I feel the mattress sink down, and I open my eyes.

"You don't mind if I watch a little TV, do you? I'll keep it low. It's easier to see from here," Tom says.

"You want to trade beds? I don't mind," I say.

"No, there's plenty of room; this is fine."

"Fine."

Tom gets up, turns on the TV, and sinks back onto my bed. I half turn to see if he still has his boots on. He does. He's on top of the sheet; I'm under it.

He turns on his elbow and faces my back. His weight shifts, closer. I roll a little over on my stomach, then shift again onto my side, a bit closer to the edge. I straighten my back so I'm no longer in a fetal position.

"How much did you spend getting here?" he asks.

"About 75," I say.

"You save your receipts?"

"Of course."

"Where'd you eat?"

"At a truck stop."

"You stop to sleep at all?"

"No; well, barely. I slept for about 20 minutes in the South of the Border parking lot 'cause my eyes burned so bad."

"Yeah, that burning is the worst."

I plump the pillow, then settle back down. "You know, I hate to be rude, but like I said, I'm way tired, so I'm gonna go to sleep now. Okay? I'm gonna stop talking now."

Tom lies there quietly smoking for a few minutes. The mattress rises slightly when he rolls over to crush out his cigarette. I'm annoyed with myself; generally I can fall asleep anywhere, anytime.

"TV bother you?"

"No. I'm so tired I can sleep with it."

"Good." His weight shifts towards me again. I pull myself closer to the edge of the bed with my left hand. Worried I might fall off, I steady myself by gripping the edge of the mattress with my fingers.

He puts his hand on my left hip. I try to breathe evenly, as if I'm asleep. Maybe he'll take his hand away if I seem asleep. Tante once told me bears wouldn't eat you if you seemed dead. I think of bears. I concentrate on slowing my breath. In—two; out—two. I'm not getting enough oxygen. My muscles tense to keep me from rolling entirely off the bed.

His palm strokes my hipbone in rhythm with my slow breaths.

Tom lost 3 fingers when his left hand was sucked into a pulley block by a runaway line. This happened years ago, before Ma got with Pa, before we joined the show. Now his pinkie and thumb are separated by a slab of soft boneless meat. Like the hands of the freak show Lobster Boy. The pointer, the curse finger, the wedding band finger, are missing. Still, I can feel them through my sweats like ice.

"Relax," he says. "Do you want a massage?" He rubs gentle circles into my hip.

"No." Sitting up now, I say, "I think I'm just overtired, so I can't relax. I think I'll go for a swim." I go to the bathroom to change again. This time I jam my toe against the corner of the door to keep it shut.

When we're on the lot, Tom and I sit on the top of the tent and talk sometimes. There's usually a great view no matter what town we're in, especially during sunsets. Tom knows everything about the circus, and he teaches me. History, trivia, everything about moving and caring for the canvas.

In the bathroom, changing into my swimsuit, I check the mirror for worn-through spots. None in any bad places. Still, I cover the tight Lycra with my tee and sweats.

One time when the show was in Long Island, we'd climbed up the mast to watch a far-off electrical storm. Sitting there on the red vinyl cupola, staring into the greenish clouds and sharp cracks of lightning, Tom taught me to count until I heard the boom of thunder. He said that's how I could tell how far off the storm was and if it was heading towards us. Every five seconds equals a mile, he said. A canvas boss has to know about weather, he said. If a storm comes up fast, we should be ready to drop the tent.

Then he told me about Patsy. How she was different. It's true. I went to their wedding and saw how different. Everyone went. We got the whole day off. Their wedding was in a church instead of the bigtop. And the reception was in her sister's backyard. Her parents had paid for it; she wore white. I've always wanted a wedding just like Tom and Patsy's. Movie perfect. I didn't know Jayson could waltz till he pulled me to the floor. Later, he admitted to practicing with Al behind the generator for weeks. He wore his ring tux, and looked so much like the groom on top of the cake. I wore a pink dress. Lacy. Since his daughter was gone, Tom let me be flower girl.

He looked at the sky and told me Patsy was the one.

I remember looking from the storm to the crowd milling below on the midway. For those few moments, sitting up there with Tom, removed from both the public and the weather, I felt real fine—like I was full from a good meal and just resting on a deep couch. Tom lit two Marlboros and handed one to me. He said, "I don't regret leaving Darlene for her, but sometimes I do miss my little girl." Then we smoked in silence, watching the movement of the storm. When he finished his cigarette, Tom laid his left foot over his right knee and bent over his potbelly. He crushed the butt on the sole of his boot. Then he put the filter in his pocket.

I imitated his actions. "You know why I do that?" he asked.

"So you don't burn the tent?"

"Yeah. Any tiny spark can leave a pinhole; that'll weaken the overall structure. 'Cause you can't pull a tent tight if you're worried about pinholes ripping into bigger ones, right? An' what did I teach you about a tight tent?"

"A tight tent is a safe tent." I recited the rule often enough to the crew that hit back ropes under my direction.

"Right. If it ain't tight, it ain't right."

Tom is proud to have a female on his tent crew. I'm proud he's proud. I can pull my own. The other roustabouts call me "Lady Man." When other shows are near ours, he takes me to their tear-downs to work along with their crew. He'll stand with the canvas boss and say how he taught me everything. That I'm as good as the men on his crew. Better, in fact, because I don't smell so bad and get in fewer fights. Tom and I have been on many trips together to other shows, so it makes sense that I got picked to drive on this business trip. He's seen me drive; he trusts me.

He doesn't look up from the TV when I dart across the room, towel clutched to my chest.

I cross the hot pebbly cement to the pool in front of the motel and lie down on a yellow plastic lounge chair, the motel towel rolled under my head as a pillow. I'm tired and I'm feeling it.

When Jayson and Tom called me into the production trailer and told me I was going on a mission, I was excited. Jayson handed me an envelope and said, "Take I-95 south till you hit Florida, then call for further instructions." There was 150 dollars in the envelope. Tom told me I had a half hour to pack and 25 hours to get there. When I asked why they were sending me, Jayson said I was the only one they trusted with so much money and Tom's blue pickup. They knew I'd come back. I had been flattered a little. I imagined this trip would be kind of like a vacation. I thought maybe Tom would take me to Gibtown or the trailer parks for retired Freaks and Kinkers. I pictured people mistaking me for his real daughter as we took in the sights of the clown college and circus museum.

But the only person we've seen is the old lady at the front desk, and she didn't ask if Tom was my dad. She didn't say anything but "Room 10." We're the only people in the motel. I have the pool all to myself. The chlorine smell soothes me; I close my eyes and sink into the chair's vinyl webbing.

I stayed in a motel once before. The Dew Drop Inn, with Jayson, the weekend of Tom and Patsy's wedding. Jayson paid. I still have the little shampoo, soap, and hand lotion. There were two beds, just like here. One to mess up and one to sleep in clean. Flush toilets and all the towels I could ask for. Jayson bought me silk stockings and garters to wear with my flower-girl dress. Al took me into town to get my legs waxed and showed me how to work the garters. I wore the stockings under my Carhartts till they ran. I still have the garters in my sock drawer.

Something touches my face. I try to brush it away, and Tom laughs. When I open my eyes his face is inches from mine, his good hand cupping my chin.

"You look like a bird when you sleep," he says.

"Does this mean I have to get up now?"

"No, we have a little time. Relax."

"Great."

"You know, you really are an attractive girl." Stale tobacco breath. He smooths my cheek with the back of his lobster hand. The sun backlights his straight blond hair so it turns a shiny gold. I look into his hair instead of his eyes, my mind rummaging for words, racing.

"I have to go swimming to wake up," I say. Stand and step quickly backwards, strip off my sweats. With my tee-shirt over my suit still, I dive into the water. Sit on the bottom, hold my breath, beat my hands upwards against the water to keep from floating to the surface. I'll stay under until he is gone, I figure. When I can't hold my breath any longer, I surface and begin swimming laps. I kick and thrash my arms, splashing as hard as I can, so all I hear is the foamy white sound of water.

Finally he is gone. I climb out the pool, pull off my wet tee-shirt, and rub myself dry with the coarse motel towel.

My wet feet print up the maroon carpet. A note taped to the mirror with a Band-Aid says, "Took the truck, gone to get concession wagon and order tent. Back in hour." I wonder how long ago he left that note. Since I haven't been swimming long, I figure I have time for a shower. Still, when I close the door, I close it on the folded-up cardboard box that the guest soap came in. This makes the door jam tight. Just in case.

The mirror over the sink reflects my naked body from the edge of my pubic hair up. Lifting my elbow, I make a muscle. You look like a boy with tits stuck on by mistake, I think. But Jay always says he loves my body. He whispers this in my ear, stroking my straight lines, sharp angles. He kisses my round shoulder caps and prominent collarbone and tells me he needs a woman like me, with strong enough arms to hold him. When we waltzed at Tom's wedding, Jayson said, "Our bodies fit together right. Don't ever let anyone else try you on."

I make the shower water hot as I can stand. My skin turns red. I cover myself with clean white soap. Maybe I should wash my hair. My hip remembers Tom's hand like a burn.

Tom is my boss. In fact, he is nearly everyone's boss. He supervises the moving and maintenance of the show; he supervises all the crews. Tom runs a tight show, no one out of line, nothing out of place. He would say there isn't room to fuck up. "If it ain't tight, it ain't right." He's taught me everything I know about tents. He gave me my job. It's important to remember these things.

I even stuck by him after he forklifted his first wife and kids off the lot. He'd locked the green-and-white Citation from the outside and left them on the shoulder of the road. By the next morning his wife, Darlene, had climbed out the window, but she never came back inside the yellow security fence. It was talked about in the cookhouse, but Tom fired Bob as an example, and talk stopped. When the show pulled away from the trailer stranded on the highway, I drove the blue pickup that used to pull that Citation. Not once did I consider Darlene holding the baby in her arms, road dirt kicked up in a swirl around her knees. His daughter ran alongside the truck for a ways, but I closed my eyes and picked up speed. It was my job to drive, not to think. Without my job, I'd be just another girl with no family and nowhere to go. I'm not so stupid that I don't know my place.

I rinse the soap from my body and lather up my hair.

The door rattles.

"Matty, Mat—you in there?" Tom is back.

"Yeah, I'm showering, do you mind?"

"No." He hits his shoulder against the door a few times, till the cardboard soap box gives way. It makes a scratchy sound sliding across the tile. The door opens, and I hear his voice inside. We are separated by the shower curtain. He says, "No, as long as you don't mind me shaving while you shower."

"Fine."

I hear shaving noises and feel the water turn cold as he fills the sink. A few seconds later, the water runs hot again, though not as hot as before.

"So I ordered the tent and got the wagon. Boy, it is beautiful. Wait till you see the paint job. We're gonna have to be real careful driving back. I figure we'll leave in a half hour or so and grab something to eat on the way. What do you think?"

My hair is done and I want to get out, but I can't figure how to do it without stepping out naked. Maybe I could grab a towel and wrap it around me. My clothes are on the toilet. I could grab them and run into the main room to change. Still, motel towels never reach from my armpits to my crotch. I'll stay in till he's done shaving, I figure.

"So'd you sleep well? Ready to drive? I'll drive first— what do you think?" His voice is cheerful and loud, but I can still hear the razor scrape over his skin.

"Fine."

"You gonna stay in there all day? You got to get ready to go."

"Well, actually, I was just waiting for you to be done shaving."

The water runs cold now, so I turn it off. I feel more naked without the water, like the shower curtain isn't really between us. I cross my arms over my chest.

Tom's arm snakes through the side of the curtain, holding two towels. "Hey, here's some towels. Don't worry, I won't look. I'm not like that."

I wrap one around my waist and one under my armpits. "Thanks," I say.

I step out the tub and take my clothes off the toilet. They're damp from the mist in the bathroom. I slide past Tom to the bedroom and shut the door behind me.

"Hey, let's leave the door open so we can hear each other."

"Fine."

Going to the far right side of the room, I check the angle of my view of the bathroom door. He can't see me, because I can't see him. Tante told me once that if you couldn't see the audience, then the audience couldn't see you. It's hard to work my jeans onto my wet legs. My still damp shoulders catch on my shirt.

"Hey," Tom says, suddenly behind me. I keep buttoning my shirt, slowly, casually.

He lifts my wet hair from my shoulders and touches my neck. A two finger touch, the pinkie, soft meat, the thumb. His good hand holds my hair. Five fingers in a fist, wove tight in my hair.

"Please. Don't." Without turning, I push at the soft empty palm on my neck.

"What? Relax."

"Just don't, okay?"

He won't stop stroking. I drop my hands in frustration. Their loud slap against my thighs startles me.

"What's the matter with you? You're real jumpy."

"I'm just tired, okay? Please stop."

His hands move down my shoulders to my forearms and rest just above my wrists. One thick and hard, one soft and childish. His breath cools my wet scalp.

"Listen," he says. "This isn't any different from what you do with Jay."

I step forward out of his grasp. "It's different. Way different. What about Patsy?"

"You never worry about Kelli."

"It's different."

He puts his hands back on my shoulders. "It's not. You tell me how it's different."

"It just is, is all." I shake off his hands and throw the damp towels in the bathroom.

"Jayson knows. He set this up," Tom calls at my wet, cold back. My eyes narrow, but I don't turn around.

"Get your stuff, Tom. You said we were leaving in a half hour a half hour ago."

Tom drives most of the way back. I lean my head against the glass and watch the trees on the interstate blur by.

I remember the conversation Tom and I had on top of the tent. He told me Patsy was his dream girl, she was who he wanted to spend the rest of his life with. He had grown away from Darlene. They'd stopped having sex after the baby. But Patsy was the one. The One.

Tom's voice breaks into my thoughts. Our eyes meet in the rearview. "You know, I'm looking forward to seeing Patsy again. Can you believe this is the longest we've been apart since we got together?"

"Yeah, that's nice." Suddenly I'm very sleepy. My head rocks against the window. I want to close my eyes.

Tom lights himself a Marlboro with his silver plated Harley lighter. Patsy gave it to him at their wedding. The truck fills with blue smoke.

"There's a truck stop in Georgia that sells fireworks cheap. Remind me to stop in there. I want to send some to my little girl."

"Yeah, I'll try to remind you," I say.

"That's my girl." He hits me on the knee with a hard open hand, so I can't mistake his touch for anything more than a slap between friends.

I count twenty mile markers before I say, "My eyes burn; I'm gonna rest them, okay?"

"Yeah; that's the worst." Tom cracks his window and flicks his cigarette in the wind with his thick yellow thumb. Sparks stream out from the butt. This is the last thing I see before I close my eyes. He's still talking. "I can stay up longer than my eyes. You know what I do when I'm driving long hours? When my eyes start to burn, this is what I do. I wait till a straightaway, and then I close my eyes and count slowly to ten. Then I open them for five and do it again. Best way to rest burning eyes. Never had an accident. Just close your eyes and count to ten, but be sure to open them again. Sometimes it's hard to. There's always the temptation to hang on to 15 or 20. Then you'd be pushing it."

August
1985

▲

Redlighting the Kid

▲

The waitress pours Jay another oily cup of coffee. She's probably in her forties, but her hair and face are done up like a high school homecoming queen. Her makeup looks clownish under the fluorescent lights. But Jay winks at her anyhow, and smiles. She smiles back. Then slips away softly in her orthopedic nurse shoes.

Sometimes I dream I'm a truck stop waitress. And Jay's a trucker. And we have a home, in one place, just us. We'd be happy. But looking at her, I can tell she's not happy. She looks uncomfortable in those nylon stockings she keeps hitching up her sagging hips. That bra she keeps pulling down to harness her unruly breasts. Mine hang free under my tee-shirt, the grit of sweat and ringdirt trapped between their curve and my ribcage.

"Quit staring," Jay says. He's about as old as our waitress, and nearly twice my age, but his years translate into knowledge and assurance. On Jay, his wrinkles soften his square jaw and hard cheekbones, gentling his strong face.

He curls over his plate, dark hair brushing solid shoulders, callused elbows resting on the table. He tears shreds of meat from his nearly bare barbecue ribs. Orange grease coats his chin, is transferred to his coffee cup, the back of his hand, his dirty pocket tee. I've already wiped my heavy plate clean and licked all the gravy from my fingers.

Though it is three A.M., the truck stop is full of men sitting singly or in groups. To me, each looks hunger-artist skinny or freak-show fat. With hunched shoulders and suspicious eyes, they protect their large plates of meat and potatoes. Fried, baked, or mashed.

We're in the Kontree Kitchen Family Dining Restaurant. This interstate truck stop is a small city: the restaurant, an arcade, rent-a-showers, and a motel. It has two stores: one for truckers, with clothes and engine fluids, tools, and girlie magazines, and one for tourists, with toothpick holders, salt and pepper sets, word puzzles and comics for the kids. Outside, six diesel and six regular-gas filling stations light up the starless night. We saw them from miles away. Big rigs pass easily under their high awnings. Entrance ramps and exit ramps, sweeping loops on and off the interstate, lead into large parking lots, big enough for double tractors to pull in and out without having to back up and risk jackknifing. Jay, the Cowpoke Kid, and me pulled in an hour ago. The CB on as always, filling the cab with chatter. It told us which parking row had what drugs, where the women were, and who wanted company. But we aren't looking for a party.

We stopped here to redlight the Cowpoke Kid. The Kid is in the rental showers, using up the five dollars Jay gave him. We should be leaving now, paying the bill at the cash register and abandoning the Kid at this truck stop.

Redlighting means ditching a roustabout on the road

during a move. It's called redlighting because traditionally when you stop at a red light, you persuade your shotgun to get out the truck. You make up a story about a flapping belly box that needs duct tape. You even hand over a roll to convince him it's for real. When the light turns green, you leave him on the side of the road, choking on dust. If you've got a soft touch, you throw a bag of warm clothes and a canteen of water out the window as you drive away. There are other variations. Like our plan to leave the Kid behind in this truck stop.

Jayson throws the last bone down on his plate. A thread of meat dangles at the corner of his mouth, and I pick it off, then show it to him before wiping it on the table. "Let's go," he says.

But I dawdle, scraping black paste from under my nails with my marlinespike. After each dig, I carefully wipe parallel streaks of soil onto my paper napkin, yet my nails don't seem to be getting any cleaner.

"I don't want to redlight the Kid," I say.

"Yeah, well, Tom says we have to. He's trouble," Jayson says.

Yesterday morning, on his favorite pillow, Jayson found a used rubber. It wasn't his. He'd spent the night with me, in my sleeper. The rubber was neatly tied off; milky semen filled the last quarter inch. Kelli left it on Jay's pillow to show him she had a lover too. By the end of breakfast, everyone knew she'd fucked the Kid.

Jayson raged out the Country Squire, through boss row, past the prop truck, the sleepers, the shower truck, ran by the nicer trailers lining performer row. The condom shook in his hand. His voice echoed under the empty bigtop. He hollered for Kelli to come out, show herself. He screamed,

"You got fifteen minutes to get off this lot!" She came running from the shower truck, hair streaming wet, her sweatshirt darkened with water she hadn't had time to dry from her pale skin. He threw her clothes out the trailer door. A flurry of tee-shirts, panties, diapers, and baby wipes spilled onto the muddy lot. Roustabouts and performers stood mixed together, waiting to see what might happen. We watched Kelli gather her stuff. She tied her things in black garbage bag bundles. No one bent to quiet J.J., who lay squalling in the grass. No one helped her carry the garbage bags to a bus stop on the double lane divided highway. The Cowpoke Kid hid behind the generator. He stared at Kelli. Surrounded by garbage bags, she waited alone, J.J. propped on her hip. Finally a Greyhound took them away.

Last night, during load-out, the Kid climbed the bare mast and threatened to jump.

Shiny posters of supper plates and lunch specials line the lemon walls. The photographed burgers and salads, soups, pickles, and slaw, look huge and bright. More like toys than food. Plastic plants hang in plastic pots over each poster. An American flag is stapled above the pickup station. The long rectangular opening reveals hairy, hardworking men, sweat soiling their white tee-shirts and staining the bandannas tied around their dark heads. One catches my eye and winks. I push my hair behind my ears and check the corners of my eyes for sleep crust. Jayson looks at the kitchen, then glares at me.

I rip my napkin into tiny paper pills, line them up along the edge of the ashtray.

"I feel kind of sorry for the Kid." One by one I push the paper balls into the ashes. "He's not a bad guy; he's just kind of crazy."

"That's the problem," Jayson says, like it's settled, obvious. He stands.

"Wait," I say, loud enough for a few heads to turn. "Can't we do the right thing for once?"

"The right thing is what we're told to do," Jay says.

"It's not that simple," I say.

"Why not?" He sits.

"Because."

Last night we loaded out in an electric storm. Thunder came so close on the heels of lightning that I couldn't even count to "one-mississippi" between the flash and the boom. The tent was down and loaded on the flatbed. The four masts, hollow 63-foot steel towers, stood naked in the field, begging to be struck by lightning.

"I'm gonna jump," the Kid yelled from the northwest mast. "You tell Kelli I love her like a sonofabitch, but a man's gotta do what a man's gotta do."

Tom grabbed me by the elbow. "You go on up and talk that crazy bastard down. The last thing we need is a suicide. That'll bring troopers for sure."

I climbed to the Kid. We stood next to each other, gripping cold wet steel, my feet and fingers numb. He was wide-eyed and shaking.

"Come on now, Kid, you don't want to die and get us all in trouble here." I spoke to him in a mother's voice, gentle and singsong. "We got to get down off this mast before Tom gets mad." I spoke like he was a baby who woke up crying with night fears. "We're holding things up. We got to move on here."

If I wanted to, I could've reached across and touched the Kid's hollow white cheeks, tucked his bleached wheat hair under his feedstore cap. His embroidered yoke shirt was soaked through, stuck to his whip-skinny back; I could count his chicken ribs if I had a mind to. It looked like his wrists could snap at any moment, like stems off of green beans.

The waitress sways through her station, a pot of leaded in one hand and the orange topped pot of decaf in the other. Her hair curls from the coffee's steam. Perspiration darkens the underarms of her blue polyester uniform. Her white apron is smeared brown and green. Tonight's special vegetable is creamed spinach; gravy's on everything.

I'm trying to explain how crazy and helpless the Kid is, but Jay keeps getting stuck on the wrong details.

"Weren't you afraid of getting struck by lightning?" he asks.

"No," I say. "I heard once that lightning strikes men seven times more than women. So I'm not gonna start worrying till I see seven men struck down." I glance at the truckers talking around the wads of meat in their cheeks. They all wear different plaid shirts, in reds or blues. No yellow, green, or purple. Cowboy or baseball hats. Boots, either engineer or cowboy. Jeans or chinos, belts with big buckles. "And I haven't seen one killed yet."

"You're cold, Baby." He reaches across the sparkle speckled green Formica and taps out one of my Luckies, then another for me. He waits for me to put mine to my lips. He lights both off a single match.

He holds a flyaway strand of my hair from the flame with his index finger. Then strokes it back in place when my cigarette has caught.

"Aren't you afraid of anything?" he asks.

"No," I answer. I don't say: I'm afraid of what you did to Kelli, of what we're gonna do to the Kid. I don't say: I'm afraid of being left alone.

"How about you?" I ask him.

"Right now, I'm afraid we're running out of time. We got to get the hell out of here before the Kid gets back." But he waits till he's smoked out the Lucky to a nub he can barely pinch between his fingers. He doesn't seem to be in a rush.

Neither am I. "You know what the Kid told me up there on the mast?"

"What? Is this gonna be a long story? We should really be going." He twists around in his chair.

"No. Wait till I finish my coffee. There's no way he's done yet."

He puts his heels up on my knees. "Okay. What?"

I massage his feet through his muddy Keds. Ringdirt crumbles in my hands.

"He told me he'd just hitched off a rodeo in Kansas, because—get this—his pregnant wife was gored by a bull."

"You're shittin' me." With a gesture so subtle I only see its result, he asks the waitress for a refill. Her shoes squeak on the linoleum. Our eyes meet over Jay's thick hair. Her breast sways towards his cheek. It brushes his shoulder lightly as she bends over his mug. He smiles and mouths thank-you at her.

When she's gone, I say, "Weird, huh? Can you beat that?"

"What a whack." Jay tastes his coffee and adds a few spoons of sugar. "You think he was gonna rejoin his loved ones in heaven?"

"No, I don't think he really wants to die. I think he's just sick of getting left behind by women. He didn't really seem to get crazy till you ran Kelli and J.J off."

Jay kicks my hands off and slams his feet onto the green tiles. "Funny. I think it's a relief to be rid of her and the damn kid. He coulda had them, far as I'm concerned. She was a pain in my ass."

His eyes wander over to the waitress wiping down the sneeze guard over the salad bar. Her rag leaves cloudy streaks on the plastic. When she stretches to hit the top with her dirty rag, her dress hikes up, revealing the dark line where her nylons turn into panties.

"You think I got time to hit the head? All this coffee, you know?" He pushes himself back from the table. The chair legs scratch against the linoleum, and my teeth ache.

"Sure," I say. "He just got in there—what?—ten minutes ago? He's a clean kinda guy; he'll be a while." I imagine the Kid washing his white feet, balanced awkwardly with one foot lifted and pressed against a bony knee, rubbing soap between his long toes. I'd bet he dries every inch of his body carefully, then stands in his BVDs, holding his damp embroidered-yoke shirt to the hot air hand dryer, so he can return the dry sweatshirt I lent him. When he changed in the truck, his hairless chest was marked with fingernail rakes, like the parallel red scratches Jay has near his right eye. I think of Kelli's long red nails. "Go on." I urge Jay towards the men's room with a jut of my chin. "He's probably blow drying his hair."

The dining room is divided into two sections. A sign blocks our view of the hall to the showers. The cardboard placard facing us says: THIS SECTION—TRUCKERS ONLY. The other side, which we can't see, reads: FAMILIES. Jay disappears behind this sign. I pick at the spiced apple ring he left behind on his plate.

When I reached the Kid at the top of the mast, he'd said, "You think I'll go to Hell if I jump?"

"How the hell would I know?" I said.

He said, "Stay up here with me a bit."

I promised I wouldn't leave him alone. He apologized for being so much trouble. Told me he wasn't raised to behave like this, that his mama didn't raise a troublemaker, raised him right, she did. It's just that things'd been going downhill for so long. I clung to the mast and tried to ignore the icy rain, the close lightning, the fact we were on the highest metal structures in a flat grass lot. I nodded and hummed sympathetically. He told me more about himself than I ever want to know about anyone. Finally he wore himself down. He said, "Okay, I'm ready to leave."

We climbed down to the safety of the ringdirt together. Together, we moved one limb at a time, maintaining three points of contact with each step, every motion mirrored. I held him to the mast with my eyes and words: I'm with you. I'm watching out for you. I won't leave you.

I suck Jay's parsley out of my back teeth, and then he's in front of me, slapping the chair. "Let's go let's go let's go!" He swipes the check off the table.

I take the green-and-white slip out of his hand and say, "I'm not leaving the Kid."

"Ah, shit, Mat." Jay slaps the table. "Now what the fuck are we gonna do?"

The waitress swings by. "How we all doin'?" she asks, cheery.

"Fine," Jay says. I hand the check back to the waitress. "I'd like some apple pie," I say.

"And for you, sir?" She smiles at Jay. He grips the back of the chair. She adds the pie to the check and looks at him hopefully. She sizes him up, from his feet, to his crotch, to his eyes. She's the right height to tuck her head under his chin, if they were to hold each other.

He unlocks his jaw and says, "Coffee."

"Nothin' sweet? I could recommend something I know you'd like. . . ."

"No, thanks. I've had plenty," he says.

She says, "Well, be sure to call me if you need anything."

Jay usually stands as if defying gravity's ability to hold him to this earth, his shoulders lifting his ribs out of his stomach, his pelvis out of his hip sockets. He generally carries himself a couple inches taller than nature intended, making the most of his five feet ten inches. Now he just collapses in on himself, plunks down in the chair, defeated by the earth's pull.

"Ah, shit," he says, rubbing his eyes.

I inspect the tabletop. Formica for easy cleanup. Gold glitter scatters over a repeating pattern of black and silver kidney bean outlines, all on a field of seafoam green. I bet the waitress can wipe away the evidence of each diner with one savage swipe of that cloth that hangs over her apron strings.

"Mat, Matty, Baby, Sugar. We have to get rid of him. Tom said," Jay says.

I sit inflexible. I'm enjoying the pleading note in his voice. Now Kelli is gone, I have more power, more pull. I know Jay hates sleeping alone.

The waitress drops my pie and the check in front of me backhanded, her body pulling towards Jayson's coffee cup. Her pour is careful and slow, like the coffee is molasses.

She lifts a porcelain cow by its tail and coos, "Cream, Sugar?" I splinter my pie crust with the sharp points of my fork.

Jay smiles and says no thanks. She replaces the cow so it's smiling at him, and sashays off.

He stares at me with tired eyes, slanted down in the outside corners, watery like an old dog's. "Since when did you get a conscience?"

I say quietly, "Just how many people we gonna fuck with, Jay? Huh? Just how many?"

"I don't know what you mean by that." He lifts the cow by its tail and it spits cream in his coffee. He won't look me in the eye.

"Yeah, you don't know what I mean," I say. But he knows. We know. People know.

Jay holds up his hand, fingers spread as if blocking my words from his face.

I toy with my pie, squishing the cinnamony gelatin between the fork's tines. I'm not really hungry for it.

Jay says, "Remember when we ditched that truck in Royalle?"

"Yeah, and so?" We'd stripped off the plates and registration and took everything that could show whose it was. We cleaned out the glove box.

"So that's what we got to do here." He reaches for the check, but I grab his wrist and hold it.

"It seems to me that all we do is move around, leaving broken shit behind," I say.

"Like what else?"

I bite the callused scar that runs from the base of my pinkie to its tip. I spit half moons of rubbery skin onto the table and push the scar bits into a little pile. "Like all these people. They come to the circus, work a bit, then fuck up. Have a baby, get pneumonia, get beat up, whatever. We leave them behind."

"Survival of the fittest," Jay says. "We cull the herd. Can't carry the weak ones. Darwin, Baby." He folds my hand into his and squeezes. My pinkie is raw where I chewed off the skin.

I pull my hand out from under his. "But we don't have to abandon them on the side of the road. We aren't animals." I disembowel the cigarette butts, pulling tobacco from paper.

"Oh?"

"I just feel like, instead of just getting rid of them, we could put them somewhere. Safe. Where they'll be taken care of." I drown cigarette papers in my coffee.

"That's not our job. Not our problem. We didn't make the Kid try to whack himself." Jay helps himself to my pie. With one scoop of his fork, he removes half the sweet insides.

Now I work on the tobacco shreds, rolling them into capsules. "What's his biggest fault? He just loved Kelli—"

"Like a sonofabitch," Jay interrupts.

"That's more than you did."

Jay throws his hands up and rolls his eyes. "I don't give a shit if he loved her, fucked her, married her, for crissakes. As long as they kept quiet about it. The point is, they went all crazy, got all out of control. We can't have that." He jabs the air with the fork. Pie bits fly off and stick to the table. Now the seafoam Formica is littered with crumbs.

The air vibrates. I check the other diners to see who's listening, who's looking at us, judging. Only the waitress smiles, tips her head towards the cashier, and says something. The cashier nods in the direction of Jay. I scratch the corner of my eye with my middle finger, and they look away.

Across the dining room, the Kid waves to us, wrinkled pink and dripping from his shower. Smiling to find us still there.

A damp moon stains his back between his shoulder blades, where he couldn't reach with his towel. He wears the yoke shirt again, my sweatshirt neatly folded in his girlish fist. The roses on his chest are faded now, the white fabric below permanently stained pink. He's got his good cowboy hat on his carefully combed hair, though the hat doesn't look fresh anymore. It used to be white straw. Since he's been with the show it's lost the feather rosette, and the sagging brim has turned grayish. A comb, the black plastic rectangle kind you get free at men's barbershops in small towns, peeks out his fancy stitch jean pocket.

The Kid sits next to me in the booth, and I slide over so our thighs don't touch.

"You want something? Pie maybe? Good pie." I spin the condiment tray so the laminated dessert card propped in the center faces him. In the tray, Tabasco, mustard, ketchup, salt, pepper, and steak sauce crowd each other. A brown crust coats the A-1 cap. Uncle Gumbo's Mo-Jo Juice, green and watery, hovers on the edge, ready to jump. The label reads: "Getcher Mo-Jo Rizin'." An alligator licks his cartoon smile at a bright-red crawfish squirming in his claw.

The Kid turns the colorful dessert card over and over in his graceful fingers. He inspects the photo of a sundae. Hot fudge steaming down a vanilla mound, a maraschino cherry on top. He grins a wide crooked smile and says, "Naw, y'all spent enough already."

Jay slaps the brim of the Kid's hat so it covers his eyes. "Naw, we-all did not. Here, y'all, get a big ole slice of pie, y'all."

"Jay, now come on. Leave him alone."

The Kid doesn't adjust his hat. He says "Naw" again and rocks a bit in his seat.

"You believe in magic?" Jay asks.

"Naw." The Kid rocks and grins.

"Naw, but you believe in God. God told you to come down off'n that thar mast or He'd damn you to Hell forever.

I reckon you're a God-fearin' man, darn tootin'. Doesn't God have something to say about fucking another man's woman?"

"Jay . . . "

"Hey, don't worry about it, Kid." Jay flips the brim out the Kid's eyes. "I'm gonna show you some magic, and magic's better than God, because it's real."

Jay sprinkles a mound of salt on the green Formica. When he has a sizable amount, he tilts the salt shaker in the middle of the pile. It rests there, hovering on the diagonal, like a plane lifting off a runway. Then he eases his face to the edge of the table and carefully blows the excess salt away from the tipped shaker with the lightest breath. A few invisible crystals hold the shaker in place. I've seen this trick before. Jay has explained it to me, though my hands tremble too much to carry it out.

The shaker remains balanced on its edge, as if caught in mid-fall. A miracle of stopped time.

"Magic," Jay says. "Better than God."

The Kid lifts his hands to clap and slaps the table accidentally with his bony wrist. The shaker falls over and spills a few grains.

"Sorry, sorry, sorry." The Kid rocks and pulls his long fingers, cracking the joints. The cashier looks over at us. Sees me and drops her eyes.

"Hey now, hey. No big deal. Okay, buddy? Okay?" Jay puts his hand on the Kid's shoulder and holds him still. With his other hand he fishes in his pockets and pulls out a fistful of silver change.

"Why don't you just go to the arcade and play some videos? They got a good strip poker game. See what you can get off the ladies, Stud. I heard one of them looks like Kelli-kitten." The Kid runs as soon as the coins contact his palm. I pinch the spilled grains in my fingers and toss them over my shoulder. Then I replace the shaker in the condiment tray.

"You're cruel Jay," I say, but my words carry no force. I could just as well be commenting on the time or the flavor of my pie.

"Enough bleeding hearts, Baby." Jay pinches my cheek. He snatches the check from under my pie plate and swaggers to the cash register.

The cashier's boot-black hair is piled high on her head, swirled around stiff like candy floss. If she came to the show, the bleacher boys would pass the word "Big hair alert." And the box-office bettys would ready tickets to move the unfortunates seated behind her to ringside.

I watch Jay's back. The muscles in his shoulder blades flex when he digs for money in his jeans. His pants are worn so thin they hang like muddy silk off his hard thighs.

He turns and winks. I'm pleased the waitress watches him heading back to me.

For a moment I consider what if he really had married Kelli? Went off to another show with her? What if he ran off with that waitress and became a trucker? What if he just ran off?

Jay makes his way back through the maze of tables, and I slow my breath, my heart, relax my mouth and eyes.

"Thought about leaving without you, Babe." He smiles.

I feel like an open wound, bleeding all over the table. "You wouldn't."

"Maybe not." He brushes his fingers against my lips and I draw them into my mouth, licking softly. He tastes like iron filings. I know what he likes.

His fingers slide down my chin, neck, and breastbone. Then he folds my hand in his. "You make me go soft, Mat."

"Yeah, that so?" I press my sneaker into his crotch under the table. I wish the waitress could see this.

Jay slips my sneaker off my foot and tilts back in his chair. His head rolls back on his neck, and his eyes close. His lips part slightly. His breathing shifts from nose to mouth.

The waitress makes her rounds with the coffeepot. When she heads towards our table, I stare at her so evil she hangs a right and heads to the other side of the dining room.

She heats up everyone's joe except Jay's. I press and stroke gently. A plate breaks in the kitchen. Jay opens his eyes, shakes his head. Surprised, guilty. Like he used to look when he woke up next to me instead of Kelli. He removes my foot from his lap. I kick my sneaker back on under the table.

He says, "Could you please explain what we're still doing here?"

"I feel kind of responsible," I say. "I'm surprised you don't." He's staring blankly at the food posters on the wall. "Maybe I'm not so surprised."

"Could you please explain why we're responsible for the Kid?" He lights another cigarette and stares at the burning ember. "This shit's gonna kill me."

I kick him lightly under the table. "Didn't it bother you at all to see J.J. leaving on a Greyhound?"

Jay looks at his hands, sagging in his lap. He doesn't answer me.

"But that was your kid." I'd wanted to say that then, and I still want to say it now. But I don't. It won't get me anywhere to anger Jay. Done is done, Tom would say. But I just wanted to hold J.J. till he quieted, till his mother dropped her useless shit and picked him up instead. I wanted to keep him, step into Kelli's place as the mother of Jay's kid.

The expression on Jay's face never changes. He simply looks tired.

The waitress ushers a large man to the booth next to us. His belly hangs low over his belt. His legs look too tiny to support his upper body. I wonder what he's carrying in his rig. Where he got it and where he's leaving it. Bread? Bananas? Auto parts? I wonder if anyone would believe what we're carrying. And where we plan to leave him.

"Well, what do you want to do with him?" Jay finally asks.

"We could take him to a hospital," I answer.

Jay slaps the table. "Aw, that's great. Let's get the authorities involved. Tom'll love that. He'll kill us." The trucker glances over at our table, then goes back to his menu.

"It's better than leaving him here, isn't it? It is better. Isn't it?"

This is my vision for the Kid. I imagine him returning from the video games: We take him gently by his elbows and escort him to our truck. On the way, we tell him he just needs a little rest is all; Tom said so. But he needs to rest in a safe place, we'll say. He'll nod his head and rock a bit in his seat, repeating those words, "Rest. Safe." Until he's convinced himself.

Jay will follow the blue hospital signs with the white H's off the highway. To some state hospital, brick or stone maybe. Strong and secure for sure. Wide sliding glass doors. The cement awning over them will be lightly creased in the exact center, divided into two broad slabs tipped upwards, like two planes taking off in opposite directions. The awning's shape reminds me of the shallow V's children draw to signify birds. A suggestion of flight, lightness, heaven. A soft white light welcomes us. The 3-D steel letters perched above this inspirational entrance spell EMERGENCY ROOM, but they don't break the magic feeling that these doors lead to safety.

We will sit in seafoam-green chairs. Walls the same color, the color of calm. Everything's sparkly clean. Magazines about good housekeeping and family circles rest comfortably in tidy racks. Here, in the paper scattered on the table, there is no bad news, no death or abandoned children. Only Lifestyles, and Funnies, and Recipes.

I will push silver change into the Kid's hand, and he will run to the shining machines for hot chocolate and cheez crackers. Then I'll say to the beautiful motherly desk nurse, "My husband and I are migrant fruit pickers. We were on our way to the next farm when we came across this poor boy on the side of the road. He seems ill. He definitely needs more help than we can give."

"The poor dear," she croons. Warm and mellow, like an actress.

"We'd help him ourselves if we could, but we got to move on, though he's been like a son to us." Tears spring to my eyes, almost natural, believable. She pats my scarred knuckles with her soft paper-dry fingers. They smell like lotion and pink liquid bathroom soap.

"Please take care of him for us."

"Of course we will, dear. He'll be safe here." She smiles a warm lipstick smile. I'm melting inside.

"Now you take care of yourself," she continues. "You look tired, dearie."

"Oh no, we'll be fine," I reassure, competent, confident, brave. Still, gratitude sugars my voice. "By the way," I whisper, so low she must bend to hear me. I imagine the fine white hairs on her cheeks, smell her face powder, the scent of grandmothers and churches. "He's crazy," I'll say softly. "Don't believe anything he says."

She'll nod and wink, all believing, all embracing, all milk and cookies kindness. I won't feel a twinge in my stomach, no flinch in the back of my neck from worry or guilt as I glide through the wide glass doors. I turn to see the Kid smiling at the nurse, sharing his goodies. They are friends; she adopts him.

That is my vision for the Kid. But already I know, watching Jay's face darken and his fingers counting off each other, he's figuring. He's figuring the extra mileage a side trip to the hospital would show on the odometer. He's figuring the hours lost here and more lost looking for a hospital. He's figuring how threatened Tom felt about the scene during load-out. And how that will translate in terms of anger and punishment and favors owed. He's figuring how much trouble he's already brought down on his head with the whole Kelli mess. The ugly triangle with me. The complicated birth of J.J. The troopers who questioned him about a crazy woman and a baby, storming through town. Kelli came back to the lot during load-out. She waved a gun, screaming, "I'm gonna kill you! I'm gonna kill the baby. I'll kill myself!" over the yellow security fence till the bleacher boys ran her off right. Then the Kid tried to jump. Jay's figuring we should cut our losses and simply clean up this mess as we were instructed.

My only lever is he won't leave me behind too. At least part of me believes this, like part of me believes we love each other. If I can find a hospital close . . . I could ask the waitress if she knows of one. I could volunteer to drive, to tell Tom, to take the blame, to do Jay's share of stake driving the next few moves. To cover up his soft spots. Say it was me who was the bleeding heart, the pussy, the girl. We'll make up a funny story about it and tell it over and over in the cookhouse till Jay's role in all this is forgotten and everyone believes it was just that crazy broad Mat who drove to the hospital in the middle of the move because she was too chickenshit to redlight the Kid.

The Kid sneaks up on the table softly.

"Hey there," he says.

Jay flinches. Coffee spills into the saucer. He sees it's only the Kid, and his shoulders relax. The Kid wears the sheepish pink grin of a boy who just spent half an hour gawking at dirty pictures. He hovers around the corner of the table, popping his knuckles and bouncing slightly on his toes.

"Ran out of quarters," he says, a giggle hiccuping through his words.

"You get to see their titties, little man?" Jay asks, but even the Kid knows he doesn't expect an answer. The Kid just wavers there, lifting his heels slightly off the linoleum, calves tensed.

Jay shakes my pack of cigarettes, and a few shreds of tobacco fall out. He crushes the empty package in his fist.

"I'm getting more," he says.

I follow his back with my eyes. For a moment I lose him in the crowd. Suddenly I'm sure he's redlighting us both. I half raise up off my seat, heart pounding, eyes raking the swirl of bodies for Jay's familiar shape. When I see him bent over at the cigarette machine, yanking out a knob, I relax back into my seat.

"Sit down," I say to the Kid. He perches delicately on the edge of Jay's vacant chair, as if ready to take flight at any moment.

His fingers play over the table debris. A torn napkin, pie

crumbs turning stale and hard already. Smudged silverware; if someone cared to, our prints could be lifted from
them and held as evidence. Tepid coffee cools in a saucer,
the cup absurdly tipped over, forgotten in the middle of
Jay's rib bones.

I tap the back of his thin hand, and the Kid looks up in
my face. His light blue eyes are soft and wet. The pale-yel-
low lashes make me think of a rabbit, but his expression is
that of a child overwhelmed. It is impossible for me to picture this boy having sex, filling a condom or a womb with
semen, thinking about following his wife or Kelli into the
Great Whatever. I can't see him doing anything but playing
with a dog in a wide field, or fishing with his daddy's stolen
pole. There should be a law against sending unfinished kids
out into adult life, I think.

"Tom's real concerned about you. He told us to take
care of you real well, because he's real worried."

"So when are we leaving?" he asks. Rocking hard,
pulling on his already cracked knuckles. "We've been here
an awful long time. Won't Tom get mad?"

"As soon as Jay gets back we'll go. Tom won't get mad.
He wants us to take you somewhere special for a little rest
before you go back to work."

"A little rest," he says.

"Yeah, a little one." I'm careful to look directly in his
eyes, so he doesn't think I'm lying.

"A rest." His fingers play piano on the table.

"Yeah, me and Jay'll take you for a rest."

The Kid cranes his neck around in the direction of the
cigarette machine. "Where'd Jay go?" he asks.

"What do you mean?" I kneel on my seat and scan the
dining room, the vending hall where he was a moment ago.
"I'm gonna see where he went, okay? I'll get him and we'll

be right back for you. Don't leave. I don't want to come back and find you disappeared."

The vending machine hall is empty. If he's left me here alone with the Kid, I'll kill him, I think. At the end of the hall I enter the truckers' store. In less than thirty seconds I've trotted up and down every Jaysonless aisle. My chest squeezes. There's a cramp in my lower ribcage. Shit, if he's redlighting me, I'll die. I'll kill him. I'll kill myself.

I run back into the dining room, past the Kid again. Like a good boy, he sits patiently at the table. Our waitress pours coffee from one pot to another at the opposite end of the dining hall. The Kid can't hear me asking about Jay, my voice breathless and shaking.

"That nice looking man?"

I'm bouncing on my heels, stretching my arm overhead to relieve the cramp. I can't catch my breath. "Yes." Bitch. Hurry.

"Well, he just stepped out." She gestures vaguely to the sliding glass doors in the vending machine hall.

I trot past the Kid, tap him on his shoulder. "Be right back. Don't leave." And I run out the door.

Jay's in the truck, motor already running. I pound the passenger side door with my flat open palm, till he reaches over and unlocks it. I hurl myself into the cab.

"You were fucking gonna leave me there, you bastard!" I scream, hitting him in the shoulder, the chest, the chin.

He fends off my arms. He grabs my flying fists out the air and holds them still and tight at the wrists. One large hand can hold both. I struggle for a moment, then realize that he won't leave without me as long as he's holding me still.

"I know you're a big girl. I knew you'd figure out what to do. You're here now, aren't you? I'm not leaving without you, am I?"

"Aren't you?" I ask.

"Would it make you feel better if I let you drive?" He releases me.

"Yes," I say. He can't redlight a driver.

We switch positions by me sliding over his lap. His crotch and my ass brush together briefly, then separate. He makes a halfhearted grab at my right breast, then settles into his seat. Pops the dash lighter in and says, "Well?"

Driving and looking for red arrows. We follow them to the next site. At the beginning of the season, Tante hung Saint Christopher and Saint Jude from all the rearviews in a fit of Catholicism. They dangle in front of the bug splattered window, sway across my blurry vision. I nod and wake, and nod again, half dreaming. I remember Tante reweaving net stockings with the skill of an old fisherman, saying, "You should see what goes on there at night; you should hear." Three scratches across Jay's cheek. Fingernail rakes down the Kid's back, across his hairless white chest. Al saying, "He showed us in the showers. That woman chews them up and spits them out." Tom telling Jay, "Don't let it get messy. Two women can get very messy."

The tires hit the rumble strip on the edge of the interstate. Jay and I both wake to the painful drone. I sway back to the road again.

"You want me to drive?" he asks.

"No. Just talk to me."

"About what?"

"Why did you stay with her so fucking long?" Now that she's gone, I can finally ask.

"I wanted to do the right thing for once," Jay says.

"For who?" I hit the steering wheel with my palms. "Look how it turned out!" I say. My stomach aches from coffee and fading panic. We are dirty, tired. He sits half a reach away from me, the backs of his arms stuck to the sweaty seat. I want to slap him. I want him to wrap me in his arms and kiss my gritty eyes till I feel safe. I want to understand why everything we touch turns to shit.

"Well, at least we're still together," he says.

The patron saints of travelers and lost causes dance crazy on their chains, jerking with each bump. They wrap around each other momentarily, then fall away. Jay and I lapse into smoking silence. He smacks me every so often in the shoulder with the back of his knuckles to point out red arrows. These whacks get softer; they turn to taps, then strokes. Eventually his arm rests behind my neck, he leans into me.

I wonder how long the Kid will sit at our table. Will the waitress clean up around him, or will she let the food sit as long as he does? Will it sit on our plates until it molds and rots away? Or until he's eaten every bone, licked every grease stain? We left him alone without money, and he will wait for us forever because he's a good and faithful boy. He will starve unless he chips the dried creamed spinach from the Formica table. Unless the waitress takes pity and adopts him.

"Play a tape," I say. "I'm fading fast."

Jay says, "Check this. He left it behind on my pillow, before he climbed the mast. What a crazy shit."

The tape whirs and crackles, then the Kid speaks to us in a mournful drawl:

"I know what you're plannin' to do, Kelli-kitten. And though we can't be together, I'm with you in my heart.

"I'm keepin' up my end of the bargain, 'cause a man's gotta do what a man's gotta do. And I love you like a son-ofabitch. When we meet in heaven, we'll be lovers in wings."

Jay plays it over and over till we have it memorized, till we can recite right along, with every twang and inflection. I know we'll play this tape in the cookhouse the same way. Every roustabout will memorize it; they'll all repeat it to one another, make it a legend, a sign. All those who know the taped message will be known as Old-Timers, those who don't will be called First-of-Mays, New-Jacks.

"Do you think she'll do it?" I ask Jay.

"She's too self-centered. Besides, she stole all my money out my sock drawer. Why would a suicide need two hundred and thirty dollars?"

"You're right."

After a bit, I ask, "You think he will?"

Jay says, "Of course he will. He's got no reason not to. He ain't got shit."

"Ah, shit." I bang my forehead against the steering wheel. I don't even know the Cowpoke Kid's real name. No one ever bothered to ask. I bang my head again. We won't ever know what happens. What he does. What we did to him.

"Ah, fuck!" I scream. There's not a word strong enough for the ugly feeling in my chest. I wish I could crawl out my filthy skin. I bang my head on the wheel. Over and over.

Jay grabs my head between his hands. He holds me still. Miraculously, I am still driving. We are still barreling down the interstate. I was hoping the red haze would clear from my eyes to show we'd flipped over, crashed through the guardrail, careened over a cliff. But we're on a flat straight road. There'll be no accidents here.

Jay strokes my hair, my cheek. "Hey now, hey. You just did your job. Done is done." He kisses my temple, my jaw. "Show must go on. Survival of the fittest."

The predawn sky is the color of a bruise. I follow three

red arrows down a bumpy country road. Saint Jude and Saint Christopher slap the window with each pothole. I rip them from the rearview and throw them to the floor. This small violence does nothing to quiet the nasty voices in my head.

A shiny white frog jumps into my headlight beam. I swerve and hit it.

"Fuck it," I say. My chin sinks to the steering wheel. I'm too tired to hold my head up. I think. Please, God . . . but then don't know what to ask for.

Jay looks out the window. "Ten points." He kisses the air between us.

August
1986

▲

Moving

▲

Jayson grips both fists on the steering wheel. Straight armed, elbows locked, back pressed into the seat. A clothespin is clamped to his left nipple. When he moves it from his chest to his lower lip, I can't keep my mouth shut any longer.

"You know," I say, meeting his eyes in the rearview mirror, "I really hate that."

"What?" He downshifts violently, grinding gears.

"That clothespin."

"Get over it, Babe." The clothespin clicks against his teeth.

The silent miles pass, marked by green numbered rectangles: 89, 90, 91, 92. Then on mile marker 93, two red arrows pointing up and one pointing diagonal right.

"There's a turn coming up. Right hand. Get ready," I say.

"Call it out," he says.

I'm his shotgun; I'm his eyes. I read the signs and tell him what's coming. The rearview mirror between us is positioned not so he can see traffic but so I can see his eyes. In this way, I can keep him awake enough so he can do his job. His job is to drive the prop truck from one lot to the next, hurtling past weight stations and troopers, making good time without getting stopped. The plates, the registration, the load weight, are all questionable, probably illegal. It's not my job to know or ask.

At one arrow up and two diagonal right, I say, "Second warning." I check his eyes in the rearview and hit him in the shoulder.

His chin snaps off his chest. He shifts the clothespin to his earlobe and winces. "Hey, I'm awake."

"Your eyes were closed."

"I wasn't sleeping."

"Sorry."

At three pointing right we turn.

Tom has taught me well. He says, "Go with what you know." He means, Never take another route. Follow the red arrows laid out ahead of time by the 24-hour man. He knows the route. If you break down on route, it's only a matter of time before you get rescued by another roustabout. If you go off route and your truck breaks down, no one else from the circus will find you. Because the circus folk all follow the same route. They all follow the red arrows.

Four empty miles pass. I light a fresh cigarette off the ember of my last and flick the butt out the window.

"Leave it open, Mat. Secondhand smoke," Jay says.

"Jay, you smoked firsthand for 30 years."

"Yeah, well, I didn't quit to catch cancer from you."

His eyelids droop. I wish for the guts to press the tip of my cigarette into his forearm. I see it in my head, the red glow, the burning hairs and skin; then I see his fist smashing through my jaw, the red pulp, the bloody lip and teeth. I study his profile and wonder what keeps us together. Many women would call him handsome. There are still times when he makes me wet with a look and a word, but more times when I'm numb and wooden beneath him. Thick muscles, leather skin. Stomach flat like a younger man's. His eyes can still get to me: round and brown; laugh wrinkles at the corners give away his age. I wonder: Is it simply that our eyes have seen so many of the same things? Or is it just that after so many nights lying under him I have become inert? Danny explained that word to me. An object at rest stays at rest, he said. I wonder if I've simply been at rest all these years.

I touch him gently instead.

He kisses the air. "I'm fine, Babe."

"You're falling asleep," I say. "Why didn't you take anything?"

"I gave it all to Danny."

"Why?" Jayson isn't usually so openhanded with his drugs.

"He's driving my truck and house. I don't want him falling asleep and wrecking my stuff."

The sideview mirror shows Danny's headlights. I look at his headlights, then look at the stars for a sign of his safety. "Star light, star bright," I chant in my head. Thin clouds threaten to smother Orion. Danny taught me to find Orion by his belt. I'll close my eyes and count to three. If, when I open my eyes, the clouds haven't covered Orion, then I'll tell Danny I want to run away with him. At three, I lose my nerve. I turn my closed eyes to the window and wish blindly on the stars for grace.

Before I met Danny, I thought grace was just a way to move: Ladies and gentlemen, watch now as the lovely

Giselle dances across the deadly dangerous high wire of doom. What style, what grace! She had grace, for sure. But she fell anyhow, last summer. Now she lives in a wheelchair, on disability, in Sarasota.

Style and grace; soft elbows, pretty hands. I've always looked to performers like Giselle and Tattoo Lou as goddesses of style and grace. When I was a child, Lou put me on back of her horses and taught me how to style my arms and smile and curtsy. Ma clapped from the ringcurb.

"Such grace," Ma said.

Now Danny taught me grace is the promise of good things to come. I could smile on that thought if I wasn't so worried about Jayson seeing, and asking. So I smile inwards instead, inside myself. Corny as it sounds, I've been smiling a lot since I first saw Danny.

I first saw him sprawled in my lawn chair outside our sleeper. He's a bleacher boy, so he doesn't get a bunk.

That morning, Al stood over Danny, hands on his bathrobed hips, his toiletries kit dangling from his wrist. "Look what the Tooth Fairy left us!"

Blond corkscrew curls, a sparse goatee. His long arms and legs looked awkward, coltish. His face open and new. I wanted to touch him. I dragged Al away by his elbow, towards the shower truck.

In the showers, Al said, "Child, I seen how you look at him. He some sweet white meat." He swatted me with his washcloth. "You go, girl. I'll talk to Jayson. You just enjoy."

Danny stayed in my lawn chair. I brought him coffee every morning. We became friends. He read to me, from paperback books about places with names like Winesburg, Ohio, and Spoon River.

Now, moving from Pittsfield to Big Indian, shotgun to

Jay driving the prop truck, I'm thinking I'll run away from Jayson the way Ma ran from Pa. Silent, at night, no trace. No note left behind to explain. A mystery. On this move I'll tell Danny, I'll convince him it's the right thing to do, it's the safest thing. Danny drives behind us, pulling Jayson's Country Squire fifth wheel with the Ford pickup. I watch his headlights in the sideview mirror.

Jayson touches the base of my neck softly.

"Are you worried?" he asks. He moves the clothespin to his left nostril. Jaw muscles ripple for a moment, then relax. Both hands grip the steering wheel again. I shiver. Where he touched me feels different, colder.

"No," I say.

"Yes you are. Don't lie."

"Okay, I am."

"Good, I'm glad we're being honest. You know how much I hate when you lie to me."

Mist dots the windows. I reach across Jayson and turn on the windshield wipers. He grabs my wrist and holds it. I remember how just yesterday afternoon Danny held my wrist close to his nose and breathed in my skin. My stomach burned like it does now. Guilt, fear, desire; all feel the same. Jayson meets my eyes in the rearview. Now his are wide open.

"I'm only worried because you know how much Danny likes speed," I say. Once Danny told me anything worth doing was worth overdoing. Tripping. Speeding. Drinking. Reading.

"That's not all he seems to like." Jay releases me and I lean against the door. I will my heartbeat to slow to the rhythmic *wump-wump* of the wipers.

The darkness outside sears my eyes. I shift my focus to the interior. Brown vinyl dashboard cracked and dusted gray with ash. Light from the speedometer dimly washing the cab green. Nothing to look at, nothing to see. Just waiting in the dark for the next red arrow. Following the preset route. My whole life has been mapped by red arrows. Now I am ready to move. With style and grace, right out of this world. Away from Jayson. His thick body fills the cab and sucks the air right out my lungs.

I twine my fingers with his and rest our hands on the cold seat between us.

"What are you thinking, Jay?"

"I'm thinking I wish you hadn't missed the show yesterday. I worried, Tom worried." Jayson slips his hand out from under mine. "Especially when he found out Danny was gone too."

He unclips the clothespin from his nostril and wraps his arm gently around my shoulder.

Leaning in toward him, I say, "I'm sorry I worried you."

Sharp pain. I jump back and slam my shoulder against the door. Jayson laughs. I slap the clothespin off the sensitive skin under my jawbone, and my finger slips through a string of mucus. He smiles as I rub away his snot with my shirt sleeve.

"I'm sorry I hurt you," he says. He takes his arm back, and I press against the door.

Cold. I slide my hand around the edge of the closed window, but feel no draft.

Again, I flick my eyes at the sideview mirror, at the steady glare of the Ford's headlights. That's the man who will take me away, I think.

According to the dashboard clock, it's 2:23. Somewhere I lost twenty minutes. I remember half sleeping, dreaming about Danny reading to me.

That's all we've really done together, read. I tried to explain to Jayson. "We're not like you and Kelli last season," I said. "It's not like we're fucking!" That really pissed Jay off. That subject was supposed to be closed, resolved, off limits. Jay hates when I throw past history in his face.

Al backed me up, saying, "It's about time Little Miss had a friend her own age, and it's perfectly innocent. Those two children just sit outside in them chairs, in full view for all the lot to see, and he's just reading away. It's too sweet."

Jayson stormed into my sleeper, scattered paperbacks across my bunk. "You wanna read so bad, read!" He slammed the door. I tried to read those bright colored drugstore romances. On shiny covers, dark men gripped full bosomed women by their tiny waists. But I couldn't read like Danny. I'd lose the meaning before I finished a sentence. The books gathered dust on my shelf. Their uselessness made me uncomfortable. Sad and sorry for Jayson. For what he didn't understand. For what he wouldn't let me have. I gave the romances to Al. I stopped waking Danny with coffee.

But he still tempted me with the books he carried in his back pocket. They smelled like vanilla. I'd open them wide and bury my nose deep in their pages. Hidden behind the shower truck, when no one was looking. "Our Lady of Sorrow" was stamped in black ink across the edges of the pages. You could only read that if you held the book shut. Where Danny went to high school. He told me about high school, and I'm sorry I never went.

In the rearview, Jay's eyes are still open; so is his window. A shiver runs through me.

"Can you close your window? You're freezing me." I pop the dashboard lighter in.

With one swift movement Jayson pulls the lighter from

the dash and throws it out the window. I stare at the hole left behind. I stick the cigarette down the hole and hold it there awhile. But it doesn't light.

"Shit, Jay, it's fucking freezing."

Jayson says, "I got to do something to breathe in here. Besides, the cold keeps me awake. Your company's worthless, Miss LaLaLand. Where's your head?" He backhands my temple.

I stick the cigarette back in the pack. It isn't worth the fight. "If you're tired, we should stop for coffee at the next truck stop. I'll keep my eyes open for one."

"I don't need coffee. I need a little attention is all. Why don't you tell me what you're thinking about."

"Nothing. I wasn't thinking."

"You're always thinking, Mat."

"I don't remember, then." I stick my finger down the lighter hole to see if it's hot at all. It isn't, or my finger's too thick to fit in far enough. I can't figure how it knows to light a cigarette if it can't light my finger.

"Talk to me, Matty. We never talk lately."

"We talk all the time."

"No." He brushes a knuckle gently down my cheek. "I miss my little girl. You're always off with your buddies. The Dan and Al show."

"What do you want from me, Jay?"

"Tell me a story."

"I'm too tired."

Jayson crooks his arm around my neck and slaps my cheek lightly. One tap for each word. "Please. Mommy. Tell. Me. A. Story."

I look out the greasy window and count three mile markers. Jayson's hand rests on my cheek. Just after the fourth mile marker, he pinches my ear, hard.

"Tell me a story," he says.

"Ow. Okay. What about?"

"Tell me about what you and Danny did when you both missed the show."

"There's nothing to tell."

He twists my earlobe.

"There's nothing, okay?" I take his hand gently off my ear and hold it in my lap.

"Okay, Baby," he says. "Then let's just talk." He moves his hand down to my knee. I reach for my cigarettes; then remember the lighter and throw them back on the dash.

He says, "Do you know what I would do if you left me, Mat?"

"No." I open the glove compartment. No matches.

"I'd look for you."

"Yeah, and?" There are no matches in any of my pockets either.

"And I'd kill whoever took you away. Because I love you. Do you believe me?"

I face him across the dark cab. His skin looks green in the speedometer light.

"Yes," I say slowly.

"You do? I'm hurt." He pulls the corners of his mouth down in a pout. "You really think I'd kill someone?"

"Okay," I say. "No."

His hand whips across the cab and grabs my jaw. His eyes look red, tired. Smaller than usual, they search mine. His fingers press deep in my bone.

He says, "Well, you should."

I swallow. Get out of this with style. Style your way through fear. Like Giselle on the high wire before her fall. Soft elbows, pretty hands. Soft voice, pretty words.

Quietly, I say, "Okay. Jayson. Honey. I believe you."

He releases my face. "Good." He pats me on the knee. Two gentle taps. "Well, then. How about some coffee?"

"I'll keep my eyes out for a truck stop," I say. I'll talk to Danny at the truck stop, I think.

Yesterday, in Pittsfield, Danny touched my wrist and I got the idea to run away. And it's true, we did touch more that afternoon when we missed the show. But not in the way Jayson thinks, and not in the way people are whispering.

I was holding the back-door flap wide open so the elephant could pass through without ripping the tent. Danny sauntered up and stood maybe too close. The blood rushed from my head to my gut, and I admit I felt dizzy when he caught my free wrist and brought it up to his nose. I had to grip the door flap tight so as not to fall over.

It's this trick he does, guessing perfumes. He learned it bartending in the Bronx. He could guess Al's smell-well in one sniff. Lagerfeld.

He said, "Something smells sweet, but I can't tell what it is."

I looked around, worried someone might see. Jacomo the clown leaned against the generator, fingers curled around a forty-ounce. Little Rozario and her brother Nunzio played with balloon sticks and an old cotton-candy cone in the mud under the horse tent. Giggling high pitched innocent children giggles. They were digging for worms. When they caught one with a balloon stick, they imprisoned it in the candy-floss cone.

I knew Jayson was in the ring, moving the elephant tub around. I could listen to the music, an upbeat version of "The Elephant Walk," and picture the whole act in my head. Ivory, her front legs thrust ridiculously through a red felt vest rimmed with gold braid, a tiny red pillbox hat perched between her great ears; Ivory standing on the elephant tub, sitting on the tub, balancing her head and forelegs on the tub. All the many ways an elephant can mount an elephant tub. And people pay for this.

I knew how many more bars of music, how many more tricks, how many more bursts of applause before the clown entrée. I know Jay would come out right after, during the overlong juggling act, to feel me up behind the generator truck till he had to go in for intermission ringset. And I knew I wasn't doing anything wrong, but thinking about Jayson made my stomach burn with shame, or guilt, I don't know which.

I said, "Danny, quit playing. Let go."

"No, wait a sec. I almost got it." He sniffed again. "Nope, I guess not. I guess you must just smell sweet naturally."

Then the elephant march ended, with whoops from the audience. Danny dropped my wrist, and I used both hands to hold the canvas flap wide. Tahar led Ivory through with a bull hook under her ear and a steady stream of commands: "Move up, Ivory. Ivory move up. Move up. . . ." Her hide scratched against the door, marking it with sweat.

"Bet you can't smell anything but elephant now," I said.

Danny tucked his nose behind my ear. I remember his breath tickled. He whispered, "Nope. Still smells good in here."

I stepped forward, but he moved with me. He spoke into my neck again. "I got a new book I wanna read you."

"Okay," I said. "Now get out of here." I pushed him away hard and hung on the door flap till Danny was out of sight.

2:47. Mile marker 162. 163. I think about Danny. I think about Jayson. I think about cigarettes. One would be great just about now. How'd Jay ever quit? He's grinding his teeth. They squeak loud enough for me to hear. 2:49. The green numbers roll over. 2:50. I challenge myself to look away until at least 3:00. To not look at the mile markers except for arrows. Numbers slow the night down. I wish Danny was next to me, reading.

Whump! Jayson's hand slaps the seat. I flinch.

"Wake up, my little Mat. What are you thinking about? You looked like you were in dreamland."

Sit up. Shake my head. Greasy brown strands fall across my eyes.

"Sorry, Jay. I'm awake."

"I don't want to miss any arrows. I'd hate it if you got us lost, Babe." He slips his hand between my thighs.

"No problem. I've been looking."

His finger works my legs apart. 168, 169. The seams of my jeans chafe against my crotch. It hurts when he presses the fabric into my skin. 170.

"How about it, Mat? How about we pull over for a quickie?" The button and zipper open under his persistent hand. He pulls lightly on my pubic hair. I'm afraid to push him away; I don't know where to put my hands. They hover uncertainly above my legs, touching nothing, making no move. I speak calmly, careful not to provoke, challenge, excite.

"Now Jay, we don't have time. We got to get there before the tent truck, or Tom'll be mad." Just stating simple facts, no emotion. No reason for anger.

His fingers dig deeper, and I worry about the ringdirt under his nails. I worry about getting the burning pee again. Tante told me it came from being dirty.

"Come on, Babe. Just a little. It'll wake us up, break up the drive." He pulls my undecided hand into his lap. He's already hard.

"Jay. Honey? Remember? Danny's following us. If we pulled over, he'd pull over too. So we couldn't anyhow. Later, I promise." I relax my hand under his.

"You think about Danny too much, you know that? You're getting soft, Mat. Don't get soft on me, or I'll have to toughen you up. You don't want me to do that, do you?" He says this quietly, moving my hand against the bulge in his jeans. "Remember where you belong, Mat."

"Sure, Sugar. I won't go soft on you, Baby." Style and grace. Soft hands, pretty words. Unzip him, stroke him. He's too big, too thick for one hand. His breaths come soft, low in his throat. Sugar. Baby. I look away from my working hands and into the reflection of Danny's headlights in the sideview mirror.

Yesterday afternoon, when Danny and I missed the show, it felt more magic than Giselle styling on the highwire. More thrilling than parading around the ring on the back of Tattoo Lou's horse. When Danny met me behind the shower truck to show off his new book, I felt my chest open up like it did at the beginning of a good story.

The air rippled with heat, hummed with cicadas. The musty spice of corn just going to smut mixed with the sour-sweet of green apples rotting in the abandoned orchard behind the lot. Danny handed me a tiny square of paper.

"Blotter," he said. I turned the tiny square over in my hands.

"It's so small," I said.

"Yeah, but it'll show you grace," he explained. We sat on the yellow security fence behind the shower truck, waiting for the paper to dissolve under our tongues.

After a while he shook my hand and said, "See you later," like he was going somewhere, but he never left my side. We waited a bit more. Then I watched the cornfield turn into a maze. Danny put his arm around me so I wouldn't wander off and get lost forever in the secret rows of corn. Some of the ears were already diseased and black; they powdered my hair as I brushed by. We walked touching, my shoulder in his armpit, his arm around the small of my back. My head pulsed; the cornstalks looked shimmery and gold. Too much. I was too happy. I felt full.

"This is magic," I said.

"No," Danny said. "Grace."

We walked from the throbbing, buzzing corn into a cool green clearing, ringed with dying apple trees. In the center, a half-falling-down farmhouse. Once white, now gray wood softening into angel hair.

We stepped through the missing door. The living room held only bits of dry grass and leaves, mouse droppings, damp corners. Dark smears on the peeling flowered wallpaper. I thought they looked like shadow pictures, the kind Pa had made holding his fingers in shapes behind a light. I thought these shadowy stains could tell stories. As if the secrets of the family who'd lived here had dirtied the beautiful wallpaper before they moved on. I moved quickly past them, dropping my eyes.

In the kitchen, I opened closets and cabinets, while Danny looked down the cellar. I pretended to be married, shopping for a house. Maybe putting away groceries in a house I already lived in.

Danny wandered about, brushed his fingertips along dusty counters. "It smells old here, like a library."

"Mmmm." I hummed agreement, too high to form words. I moved in dreamtime. I thought: This is the soft place where the past and present bump against each other.

Any moment, Ma could walk through the kitchen, folding clean flowered dish towels over her arm, saying, "I thought you might need these. They were a bargain."

I tested the faucet. It coughed, then turned into a worm. I backed up against Danny. He smelled like soap and old books.

"You were going to read me something. Your new book. Let's go upstairs, where it's light."

Upstairs we found a white porcelain bathtub.

"Look, it has feet!" I said. Each corner sat on a claw foot holding a ball. I crouched on my haunches and traced the tub's feet. I wondered why a lion had magically turned into a tub. Maybe being a tub was his punishment for trying to run away. His porcelain legs couldn't take him anywhere anymore. And his head was completely missing. I felt like I might cry.

Danny interrupted me. "Wow, check this, man. Cool." He picked bits of broken glass off the windowsill and held them to the light. Red, yellow, and blue stained the white tiles. In his hands, the pieces blossomed into vases, dishes, bowls.

"I wonder if he lived here." I was still stuck on the mystery of the lion tub.

"Who?" Danny put the glass back carefully. I wondered if he worried about the owner returning, angry that his glass had been touched, moved.

"The lion," I explained, pointing to the frozen feet.

Danny knelt beside the tub. He leaned his hand against the curve of porcelain and tipped forward on his toes. A paperback slipped up from his back pocket.

"This tub feels nice and cool," he said, straightening. Forehead shiny with sweat. Smiling. "I think I'm gonna take me a bath." He slipped the book from out his back pocket and lay down in the tub, in the carved-out body of the tub lion.

"You gonna join me?" His arms and legs draped over the sides.

"There's no room." My chest squeezed inside me; I touched my sternum to see if it had collapsed. I wished on it. I wished that this was real.

Danny patted his stomach and smiled. He scooched back a bit to make space between his thighs. "There's room," he said. "These old tubs were made for two. Save on water that way."

I eased myself into the space between his legs. Held myself upright, contained. Not touching his inner thighs more than necessary. My shoulder blades ached from sitting so tight.

Danny stroked the back of my neck, my shoulders, like I'd seen Tattoo Lou groom her horses. Eventually, when I stopped thinking of Jayson, the stiffness in my lower back gave way. My shoulders slid onto his chest. He felt so warm compared to the cool dry porcelain on my forearms. I wanted to keep sinking into his warm chest until I was totally inside him. Like falling back slowly into a warm pond. I'd float under his skin, like floating under water. Wrapped inside his body, I knew I'd be protected. The world couldn't touch me through his skin.

"Dreamy?" He touched my cheek so soft, with just his fingertips.

"No," I said, and I reached for his hand and pulled his arm across my stomach. Jayson used to hold me like that, just holding to hold. Now it seems there's always a reason; whenever he touches me, touching always leads to more.

Danny said, "I want to read you something, okay?"

"Fine."

His hand lay solid on my collarbone. "Yeah? That's not shit; that's grace."

A blue sign dotted with white reflectors snaps me back to the truck.

"Truck stop. Quarter mile." I tap Jayson on the shoulder.

He twitches. "Yeah. I'm awake."

"I said, there's a truck stop coming up. Start signaling now, so Danny knows we're pulling over."

"Danny, Danny, Danny. Dannydannydannydanny . . . "

I put my hands over my ears. Jayson's laughing now. And I wish on the headlights behind us. I'm just wishing Danny safe. I don't know what else to do.

While Jayson walks the rows of parked trucks, looking to cop, Danny and me wander through the truck stop store. Past rows of colorful plastic coffee mugs, mirrored naked-girl mud-flap silhouettes, Naugahyde cowboy boots. At the country music section, I decide it's time. I tug the back of his tee-shirt.

"I want to leave with you," I say.

He turns around, holding a cassette. *The Best of Conway Twitty.* "But you're Jayson's shotgun," he says.

"I don't mean driving. I mean leaving." I twist the bottom of his shirt around my finger. He pulls my hand away, but his tee-shirt is already stretched out in a wrinkly point where my finger has been, twisting.

"Now, chill. Chill. I'm not getting what you're saying."

I know I have to work fast here, so I tuck my fingertips inside the top edge of his jeans. The skin on his hipbones quivers under my touch, a good sign. I know I've got him if I do this right.

"I'm saying I don't want to be with Jayson anymore. I

"It's by Elizabeth Barrett Browning." His v
heard, half felt, rumbled through my shoulder blad

"She dead?" I asked.

"I don't know. Does it matter?"

"Guess not."

"Okay now, stay awake."

"That part of it?"

"No. Now, this is: 'How Do I Love Thee,' by
Barrett Browning." He said this in his reading voic

"Wait—can you read it without all those 't
'thou's and say 'you's instead?"

"Okay. So. 'How do I love you, let me count the
Danny shifted so the book rested on my stomach ar
rested on my shoulder. His skin smelled salty, v
afternoon sun turned the tub gold, then pink. I
thinking: I could die now.

Later, after the show was long over, and som
probably Tom, had laced the tent shut against
wind, Danny and me lay in the clearing and smoke
I'd found tucked in my Luckies. My head rest
stomach and rose and fell with his breathing.
breathe in his rhythm. Overhead, the stars forme
in the broken web of apple tree branches.

I said, "Did you ever notice how the stars ma
when you look at them a long time?"

Danny said, "Yeah, I see that. If I could keep
focused in the right place and get them to sta
moment, I could read the words, too." He brush
gers through my smut-dusted hair and said, "I
got messages sometimes. The stars."

I reached up and twined my fingers in his hair
bunch of shit, Danny."

want to be with you." I work my fingers slowly across his smooth abdomen. Whisper up into his neck. This is what I do with Jayson when I want him to be nice. This is what Al taught me about men. Where to touch them. How.

"Now wait a minute." Danny pulls my hands away and holds them at my sides. The cassette pokes into my wrist-bone; it is still in his hand, pressing into my skin.

He says, "If we got together, we'd have to leave the show. Jayson and Tom would run us off the lot."

"That's what I'm saying. They're gonna anyhow. Now that we got caught missing the show. I've seen them run their own women and children off like it's nothing." I remember Tom's first family, abandoned on the side of the road; Jayson, blank faced, watching Kelli and his son boarding a Greyhound. "Danny, let's just leave before it gets ugly. Let's run away before they run us off."

"Hold on." He puts his hands on my shoulders like I am actually running away this very moment. "We can't just up and leave. Got to plan. Make plans. Plans, man." He taps the tape against my cheek. I grab it from his hand and throw it on the shelf. Plastic clatters against metal, loud. The cashier looks up at us, then back at her *Cosmo*.

As if we haven't just been speaking, touching, Danny saunters off down the aisle, brushing his fingers across each item.

I trot after him. "What's to plan?"

He stops short, and I bump into his back. His hand hovers over a display of state shaped air fresheners. The kind you dangle off the rearview mirror. Each detailed with the capital, flower, major exports, and state bird. He picks them up, one at a time, and holds them to his nose.

"Cherry . . . lemon . . . patchouli . . . cherry . . . pine . . . pine . . . lemonlemoncherrypine—"

"Danny!" I knock the green pine Arkansas from his hand.

He looks down at me and says, "Money," like it's another smell, in the same flat voice.

"Danny." I say his name soft, trying to sound like how I feel about him, only I can't feel much but scared right now.

He continues, not hearing me. "And I can't drive away with Jayson's trailer. That's stealing." Already he's floated past the snowball scene paperweights and souvenir tooth-pick holders. Picking up speed. Past the magazines, tools, lighters.

I follow him into the clothing section. Rotating islands of flannel shirts and extra-wide jeans separate us.

"Okay, then," I whisper across a rack of negligees. "We'll plan. We'll plan to leave next lot. After set-up. They're gonna run us off, Danny."

"Okay, Mat. Next lot. Whatever. But we got to get Al a going-away present. Us going away, I mean. Not him. Okay?" He speaks quickly, shooting hangers around their metal racks from one hand to the other.

"Going away. Going away. Going . . . " He holds up a hal-ter top made out of men's Fruit of the Loom briefs. It has a rose and the words "Country Music Momma" written across what should be the butt area in sparkly puff appliqués. "He'd like this." Danny struggles to get the underwear over his head, but the hanger is still clipped to it, closing off the neck opening.

The lady at the cash register says, "You gonna buy something, mister? Or just play?"

"Just play. Okay? O-O-O-kay!" He's howling like a dog, one arm through a leg hole. His head caught in the butt, hanger in his hair. The fabric stretches across his face and moves when he howls, "O-O-O-kay!"

"You're speeding, Danny, aren't you?" I help him back

out of the underwear. His face emerges, pale and bluish under the fluorescent lights.

"No. Not. Totally fine. Of course." He heads for the cowboy boots. "You know how many naugas died for these?" he screams, shaking a pair towards the cashier.

I grab for his wrists. "Put those back. You need downs." I hold his arms at his sides. His grip releases, and the boots drop to the linoleum. "We got to get you something," I say. "Maybe I should drive."

"Totally fine."

"How much did you take?" I back him against the magazine rack.

"You know. Whatever. What Jay gave me."

"Shit, Danny. How much was that?" He's scaring me now, real bad.

Danny takes a deep breath and lets it out slow. The air seems to waver, vibrate, when he exhales. He holds my hair gently away from my face, scooped into a ponytail. With his other hand, he brushes at my forehead, as if he can wipe away my frown lines. "Mat, man. Chill. Did I ever tell you about grace? Listen. Father Reilly used to drink in the Bronx store till he was ready to fall down. But nothing ever happened to him. He said, 'God takes care of little children and drunks.' And he's right. That's grace."

"But, Danny, you're not drunk. You're fucked up."

Danny pulls me to his chest; presses my face into his hot damp shirt. I turn my head to breathe. "You think God makes a difference between drunk and drugs?" he says. "God don't make a difference. God takes care of little children, drunks, and . . . druggards. Drunkards and druggards. Children, drunkards, and druggards. That's grace. I got grace."

"Don't worry, Mat. He's fine." I start at the sound of

Jayson's voice behind me. Danny pushes me away.

"I wouldn't dose my buddy." Jayson slaps his hand on Danny's shoulder and guides him towards the door. "He's driving my vehicle, my house. Right, man?"

"Yeah, man. Fine. Driving fine." Danny jingles keys in his hand.

At the vehicles, Jayson says, "I think my man should take the sharp end. You want to go ahead, Danny boy?"

"Yeah. Fine. Totally awake. Ready to go." Danny climbs into the Ford. And I just stand limp near the fender.

I just watch Jayson say, "Hey, man," and hold out his hand, fingers closed in a fist. "Hey, man, I got something for you," he says to Danny. And Danny reaches out the window, and Danny takes whatever Jayson drops in his hand.

"Thanks, Bud. Later." Danny revs the Ford, waves.

I hunch under Jay's arm now. It feels too tight, too heavy around my neck. We head for the prop truck.

3:27. I realize we've lost Danny's taillights. Jay says, "Don't worry, he's fine. He's just setting his own pace. This truck can't keep up is all." He strokes my cheek and says, "He'll be okay, I promise."

The road and the night drag. 3:48, 3:52. Jay has given up on the clothespins and now chews caffeine candies instead. Enerjets, the yellow package says. I don't read the rest of the small words. Twice now I've caught him closing his eyes and counting to ten on straight stretches of road. Once I remembered to shake him awake. The second one he came out of on his own.

Me, I slip in and out. I see black shapes that I know aren't real run across the road. My eyes feel dry, but they tear constantly, giving a halo to any light we pass, blurring the shiny white letters on the green exit signs. In and out.

I'm in the cab, tapping Jayson and looking for arrows; in a silver diner, serving truckers' early-morning coffee, a gold wedding band flashing off my ring finger as my hand moves swiftly over green Formica; eggs, toast, and hashbrowns.

Jay slaps himself hard; four slaps, two each side. He rolls down his window and howls into the damp blast of wind. I stare at the broken white line that divides and multiplies, that dances down the asphalt. I stare into the white guardrail ribbon streaming past and see the Shasta Danny will buy for me in a non-mobile-home trailer park. I can see the painted white stones I'll line our garden with, and the barbecue, and the children's bikes sprawled in the gravel.

This dream fades with the rising sun.

"The sun, already," I say. Surprised. It's early. Too bright. Too localized.

"Baby, we're heading west," Jay says. He lays his hand on top of mine and holds my fingers as we drive into the false sunrise.

Half a mile, round a dogleg turn in the highway, we see the burning Country Squire.

Jay slows to a stop, 500 yards off. It burns across two of the three lanes, billowing greasy orange flames. Black smoke pours out, like an oil can spilling upwards. Heat ripples the air. The trailer lies on its side, the Ford's front tires propped on the guardrail of the median strip. The trailer is twisted and scarred from rolling.

"Shit," Jay says. "Don't look." He tries to shield me, holds my face to his chest. But I squirm away. I want to see.

He says, "Propane blew."

Carpet, aluminum siding, curtains, upholstery, all blown out and tangled. Melting and burning. My heart rises to my throat and I taste my last meal. I swallow, and my heart drops from my body. I could die now, I think. I can't see Danny.

"No!" I scream. I hurl myself from the cab and fall on the hot pavement, palms scraping open, knees bleeding. But all I feel is the sucking hole where my heart used to be.

Jay's at my side, helping me to my feet. Holding me back. I wrench my arm out of his grip and run towards the fire; a blast of foul air slams me in the face. Eyes and nose streaming, I scream at the flames, the sky, Danny's useless grace. Screaming without words. Mindless.

"Mat, Matty, Mat ... hey now ... Mat." Jay pins my elbows behind me; my shoulder blades grind. We struggle, me straining towards the fire, he holding me back. We pull against each other till I'm pulled to my knees. He lets me fall over on my side, curl up in a ball. Rock myself. Sorry, Danny, sorry. Sorry, sorry. I open my mouth to say this, but only a hiss of air escapes my tight throat.

Eventually Jay picks me up off the road. Gently. He walks me back to the cab, lifts me inside. Like I'm a child who's fallen playing, or a fragile old woman with senile bones. I don't struggle now. I feel hollow. No fight left. Nothing to fight for, now.

We sit in the cab, watching, shoulders touching, eyes recording the burning. Ours was the first vehicle to find Danny. Traffic slowly piles up behind us. I've never been in the front of a traffic jam. Does this qualify as a traffic jam? Not many cars out at this early hour ...

"I can't ... " I've run out of words. Slipping my hand under my shirt, I touch my sternum. My skin still feels warm. My heart is still there, beating. Jayson rests his arm across my shoulders, and I lean my forehead against him. I think of Tom's advice for drivers during moves: Go with what you know. He means don't take risks. You might get lost that way.

At least I always know Jayson.

"I know," he says. His words blow into my hair and vibrate through his ribs to me. "I'm sorry, Baby . . . sorry." I want to disappear into his chest and never think or feel again. "I know he was your friend," he says. "I know how you feel about him. You want to cry some more? Go ahead. Cry. I'm sorry, Baby. Hey now, hey . . . I love you; I love you, Baby."

We're drinking coffee in the cookhouse, and the move is going slow. Outside, bleacher boys struggle with bleacher boards and stringers. Shorthanded, they haven't finished the grandstand yet. Tom, Jayson, Tante, Al, and me watch through the clear vinyl walls of the cookhouse tent; twelve sections of blue and yellow sidewall lie scattered around the bigtop. We're waiting for the bleacher boys to finish, so we can put up the wall.

Early morning sun bakes the cookhouse, making the air heavy and hot. But I hold my coffee with both hands, needing the warmth. Eventually a rainbow sheen forms across its cooling surface; it reminds me of an oilslick.

Tom stands at the door, staring into the lot. A forklift loaded with seatback risers rumbles by and carries off half his sentence ". . . something. Sure is something."

"Yes," Tante says. "We'll need to take up two collections."

Al hovers over the table, one hand on his cheek, the other holding a coffeepot. He wears his red-checkered apron. "My Donna Reed look," he calls it. I don't know who Donna Reed is. He's talking, saying, "This reminds me of the time Giselle's trailer unhitched itself and drove up alongside Pietro. Propane blew. He said he could see sparks flying from under the tanks. Same thing. Remember? 'Cept that one beached itself on the median and Pietro kept on going."

Al wanders around the table with the coffeepot, but no one has drunk any, so there's none to pour. He says, too cheery, "We got up a collection so fine, Miss Thing made out!"

"Poor girl," Tante clucks. She crosses herself.

Tom backs away from the door. "Troopers say he died on impact. Dead before he burned." He offers Marlboros all around. Al places one next to my hand. It rolls towards me and bumps my fingers. I let it rest there.

"No suffering. A blessing." Tante's hand flutters over the white web of scars on her arm. Her good eye tears. She knows burning, suffering. She drifts off somewhere; we all do. Then, "Two we'll need. One for Jayson; one for the funeral. Collections, I mean."

"There may be family. Is there family?" Tom asks, though he holds whatever paper trail exists for crew.

Al fishes Virginia Slims out his apron and throws the pack on the table. Times like these, this is what people offer. Coffee and cigarettes. And talk. Al is telling the story of Giselle's trailer again. ". . . and I remember Pietro said no amount of money or nooky Girlfriend could give him was worth the fear that rose up inside when he saw that trailer pulling up next to him, dragging its sorry propane ass." Al laughs, then puts his apron to his eyes. "I'm sorry, I can't help it. You should've seen the expression on Pietro's face when he told the story."

Jayson says, "How about the time the Deere dropped off the equipment hauler? Just rolled itself right off the flatbed onto the Volvo behind? Motherfucker wasn't strapped down right!"

Al giggles and Jayson smiles.

Tom tilts back in his chair, a tight grin stretching across his lips. "Godalmighty, I had to do some fast talking that day. Who was the idiot driving?"

"Charlie," I say. How familiar this all is. Comfortable. Tell a story, retell it, top it. Drink coffee and smoke. How many times have I been here, doing this? Telling and retelling. There is always work to do, tents and shows and moves. Danny is just another story to tell between work.

Al interrupts my thoughts. "Whatever happened to Charlie?"

"Got picked up for drugs in Kentucky. Turned out he was breaking probation," Jayson says.

"Good guy, used to work tent crew," Tom says. And I think: There's always someone to replace; someone's always leaving. But the work gets done. I look out at the bleacher boys, working their way round the seats.

"You hear about that show that caught a storm? In Italy somewhere, I think," Jayson says. "In last month's *Circus Report.*"

I look at Jayson and think about the first time I saw a real Christmas tree. I'd just turned twelve that year. After smelling real needles, touching real bark, the plastic tree Pa put up in our Airstream became garbage in my eyes. It used to be beautiful to me, because plastic was all I knew. But it became trash next to the real thing. I understand now why Ma left Pa.

Jayson tells the story. "They had pictures and everything. Tent wasn't fully up, so when the storm blew in, it flew. Sidepoles through trucks. Really. Some guy got impaled."

"I always said, 'A tent without wall is an accident waiting to happen,'" Tom says, again. Gazing at the sidewall strewn about the tent.

I shake a Virginia Slim out of the pack Al left on the table. My violent movement sends the Marlboro at my fingertips rolling to the floor. I'd forgotten it was there.

Everyone looks away from Tom's wasted cigarette; and I hide it under my foot as I bring Al's to my lips. He reaches across with his lighter. "You're welcome, Miss Zombie."

"Tired is all," I say. My brain's replayed the fire so much it's become white noise.

Tante scrapes her chair back from the table. "Well, enough gloom and doom," she says. "We need to talk moola. I say we need two collections." She holds up a legal pad with a line drawn down the center in purple crayon. One side says FUNERAL in red capital letters, the other, JAYSON, in blue.

"You see, we have to pay for Danny." She points to the FUNERAL side.

"Unless there's family," Tom interrupts.

"I thought we went through this already—no family. And two, we got to help Jayson out."

"Don't worry about me any," Jayson says. "I wanted a new truck and trailer anyhow; insurance'll pay." I look up at him, my fingers pressed to my lips. Holding my mouth shut. I can't think on this right now.

Jayson continues. ". . . and I packed everything important of mine in the prop truck."

Something by the steam tables hisses. Tom stands silently and slips out the door. A cloud passes overhead. Shadows disappear, come back. Someone drops a bleacher board, and Al says, "Well, lucky you. But why'd you pack . . . ?" Tante coughs quietly.

". . . Excuse me," Al says, running to check the oven. It is empty.

I watch the ember on my cigarette grow long, change from red to gray, and fall to the floor.

Far off, Jayson speaks. He's touching my arm, stroking

my face. "Mat, now, Baby. Don't. It's not what you're thinking."

I wonder. Can I scream now? What if I started screaming? Could I please scream now? Could I just please start
screaming and never stop?

"You got to believe me. I love you so much, Baby."

My ribs crumble and fall into my stomach. I'm far away,
floating in that soft place, in dreamtime. I barely hear
Jayson threatening.

"You're pushing me. Don't push me, Mat . . . "

Faint and distant, Al comforts, Tante explains:

"Accidents happen . . . please . . . no more trouble . . .
please, you two . . . "

Any moment, Danny will come back and take me to our
Shasta in the non-mobile-home trailer park. Any moment.

The filter burns. When I look up, everyone is gone.

I wait quietly on the ringcurb while Tante scatters
Danny's ashes in the ringdirt. He's been cremated at my
suggestion. I hated the idea of Danny underground, cold
and dark. Tante's black tunic drags in the sawdust and dirt
as she shuffles around the ring. No one else has stayed to
watch.

Fingers pressed to my breastbone, I will my heart to
slow, to stop. I count the seconds between shallow breaths.
Tante reaches into the plastic urn, lets the gray dust slip
through her webbed fingers, and reaches again. Her movements are slow, and crooked. She bends to her task; her
white hair sways at her waist. It spreads across her thin
shoulders like a shawl. Falls across her blind eye, covers
ropy scars and papery flesh. Finally she turns the jar over
and taps the sides, releasing a gray wisp. She claps her

hands three times to clean them, then joins me ringside.

My lungs feel so bruised, my heart feels so swollen against my ribs, I find it difficult to draw enough breath to ask, "Tante, what should I do?"

She rocks on her skinny hips, twists her hands in her skirts. One eye stares blindly at the bandstand. She's thinking.

Finally, "Jayson knows nothing?" she asks.

"What's there to know? Nothing happened, really." I realize I'm telling the truth. Nothing ever really did happen between us, really. I lean over and brush my fingers through the ringdirt. Remember the ashes, withdraw my hand.

"But you would have left?"

"I don't know. There were no real plans."

Tante touches my arm gently. She says, "Matilda."

Her knowing tone annoys me. She has to help me. Al is useless, too scared to say anything. Tom is too busy backing up Jayson; an accident, happens all the time. I know she sees the truth. I know she knows what to do. Who will help me if she won't? I want to shake her, squeeze her knowledge out and shoot it into my veins.

"Tell me what to do," I beg.

"Do?" She smiles, strokes my skin with her soft, dry fingers. "You do nothing now. You done enough. You made enough trouble already. You stay till God's done with you. Till God chews you up and spits you out." She speaks gently, as if giving me good news.

"I don't think I can."

She presses her bones into mine. "You can. You're strong like Assaad." She thumps her chest. "The lion." Her hand returns to its perch on my arm.

I try to shrug her off, but her fingers grip tightly. Gray under the nails.

"Matilda, listen. When I was hurt too many times by my husband, I went to Oomeh and told her I couldn't take his shit no more. I was gonna leave." Her fingers stroke the cobweb markings on her neck and cheeks.

"I don't want to talk about that," I say. My skin is still young, unlined. It feels firm beneath my fingers. Smooth and soft. Men still want to touch me. I still have both eyes. I have eyebrows, eyelashes. My lips are still full and pink. My hair, deep brown, falls past my shoulder blades in a thick braid. I'm still whole. Only my hands are scarred.

"Don't talk," she says. "Listen. Oomeh took me to the place where the mountains came to the desert. On one side green mountains, on the other flat brown sand.

"She pointed at the trees in the desert. They were twisted by the wind and short because the dirt there was too dry. Oomeh said, 'You are like those trees, planted in a hard dry land. You want to be like those.' She pointed at the tall, straight cedars on the mountain. 'But you can't pick up your roots and move from the desert where you were planted. You must learn to survive. Suffering is good for the soul. Yes? Make you strong." Tante squeezes my biceps and smiles.

"Oomeh said, 'Be like the trees in the desert. When the wind hits you, twist with it. If you think it is gonna knock you down, send your roots deeper. Deep roots give you strength. Bend to the wind, yes—but this is only above-ground. Go deep underground for your strength.'"

I shake off her pressing hand and unroll my Luckies from my sleeve. "That's a bunch of shit, Tante."

"Yeah, that so?" The old lady stands. "Well, shit is all

some of us got, Matilda. It's what you got." Tante tucks the urn under her arm and limps up the aisle. A brief flash of daylight brightens the tent. Then the door flap drops behind her. Dark again.

I walk around the empty bigtop. My steps echo on the raised wood hippodrome track. Overhead, dots of white daylight shine through pinholes in the blue vinyl. Like stars. The gold velour curtain under the bandstand stirs with a breeze I don't feel.

Red, yellow, blue, white. Vinyl, wood, steel. Lines, cables, grommets, and shackles. This is how I will fill my days. Work. I know this. Go with what you know.

I lean against the cool steel slope of a quarterpole and extend my arm with the gestures Giselle used to make on the wire to keep balance. Soft hands, pretty elbows. Style and grace. She always looked so in control. No one knows why she fell. An accident.

Giselle can't dance across a wire high over our heads anymore, but Tattoo Lou still runs her horses around the ring. Jayson, handsome, tuxedoed, will wrestle the elephant tub through the ringdirt so Ivory can balance her hindquarters on top, Tahar's knee gripped in her gentle mouth. Daisy Darling stops our hearts every time she dangles over our heads on her silver cloud swing, her purple sequined bikini throwing stars around the tent. The mysterious turbaned Sambuca will contort his twisted limbs till he fits himself in a suitcase. Jacomo the Clown will make the audience laugh blowing rainbow streamers from his red mouth. The Human Pincushion will pound a spike up his nose, gargle swords, pierce his arms with gold needles. Salvatore Diablo will gulp blazing torches, swallow dazzling fireballs. And Fabrizio, splendid in red riding jacket and black top hat, will stride across the ring, master of it all. With a majestic sweep of his arm, he directs all eyes to the spectacle, the wondrous extravaganza. But he won't sweep his arm at the ringdirt. He won't mention the dazzling fireball that swallowed the roustabout.

My eyes fill. I make a fist and punch myself in the stomach, hard. Again, harder.

Again. Until the tears stop.

Two days later, the show is moving again. One of the last on the lot, I stand where the bigtop once stood. There are few signs we have been here at all. A circle of holes left by the stakes. In the middle, under my feet, the ring. A raised mound of dirt, sawdust, and ashes.

At the center of the ring, I look at the sky. The stars don't make letters, don't spell anything. No message. I look for a long time. I look until Jayson calls me.

March
1987

▲

Tattoo Lou's New Act

▲

These are the last days of winter quarters. I don't need a calendar to know this; I can feel the tight monotonous schedule of maintenance breaking down. The air smells of last snows, last repairs. Our skeleton crew steps out the hangar for cigarettes more often. Some days are warm enough to leave the doors wide open. Damp green winds twirl dust devils, dirty feathers, and chipped paint around the hangar floor. We take off our outer layers while working. We smile more, joke more; the bottoms of our feet itch in woolen socks. There's a tug in my guts for driving. Last fall I was so ready to stay in one place; now I'm jumping out my skin to move.

Two weeks ago, we set up the rehearsal tent in the field between the cracked runways. Performers trickled in, making a trailer circle around the back entrance. Suddenly there are children to shoo away from sharp tools and poisonous solvents. Outside, under the cold March sun, Tahar's elephants sway on their chains; Tattoo Lou's horses huff silver clouds into their freshly sewn and spliced yellow-striped tent. After a winter of the same 12 dirty faces, I'm happy to see new ones. The hay man delivers; boss wives, full of spring goodwill, bake us cookies. Strange new performers gossip in French, Italian, Arabic, Spanish. They scold their daughters away from the hangar and sleepers and rough crew.

These are signs of the season beginning. The Porta-John thaws and stinks. Water runs through the all-winter-frozen shower-truck hose again, and we can wash ourselves and our clothes. Laundry lines appear, flapping clean shirts. I feel light. Now Jay is back, I won't have to sleep with one eye open and one hand on a sledgehammer handle. No more lonely roustabouts breaking in to warm up next to Al or me.

My schedule eases up. This morning I just have to air the tent out after horse practice so the place doesn't smell like a barn for the Flying Cordovas. I don't need more than a cup of coffee and a couple aspirin for that. Tattoo Lou got up a new act in Sarasota; every day now she works her horses hard, perfecting their moves, the lights, the props, the costumes.

In the cookhouse, I ignore Al till I have a large mug of black coffee burning my fingers.

Sitting tenderly, so as not to rock my aching head, I still spill my coffee. I wipe my hand on my Carhartts and get a Lucky out the bib pocket.

"Well, Miss Thing decides to grace us with her presence," Al says. "Do you know what time you got in last night? Or should I say this morning?" He cuts from behind the steam tables and saunters over. He sniffs my hair. I wave him away.

"Are we a brewery? Because I do smell yeast. Indeed. Did you get smashed last night, or is that just an infection?"

I blow smoke in his face, and he moves away.

"I was with Jay. It's been a while. You got a problem with that, Ma?"

He looks like a cat with a mouse in his cheek. "Oh, you mean that stunning man who just had breakfast with Tattoo Lou?" He swats my throbbing head with his greasy potholder.

"He's working out the props for her new act. Now just"—I massage the tight lumps over my ears—"shut up."

Al drops four extra-strength Tylenol and a warm can of Blatz on the table in front of me. Brooklyn's finest.

He snaps his fingers heavenward. "Girlfriend, you out of control." He sits in the chair opposite me, but I stare at the beer instead of meeting his eyes.

Each pill seems too big for my throat, which has somehow shrunk overnight, but the beer goes down nicely.

"What the fuck, Al. I'm hurting here, and you're talking shit before I got a full cup of coffee in me."

"Well, I think he's working more than her props, but you didn't hear it from me." Al crosses his legs and looks off into the hangar. Rectangles of dusty morning bleach the gray cement. A pigeon flies from a steel beam to a shattered work lamp. Another gray feather, another stream of chalky shit, hit the workbench. Every tool has been tarred and feathered by the birds.

My jaw feels like it's been shoved into my ears. "Well, I know where he was last night, Al, so just shut your hole."

I stare out the clear vinyl cookhouse walls at the unfinished projects we've simply given up on. The old Deere is still in pieces; the new cabinets for the shower truck will be left behind to mildew one more season. The trucks sport pink patches of Bondo, still unpainted.

Last week, while Jay was still in Sarasota, I filled the dents in those cabs, prepping them for new paint. Tom was hiring. He sat in a steel cookhouse folding chair in the middle of the wide hangar, about ten feet off from me. He'd slid the giant hangar doors open just enough to let the single file of applicants pass through one at a time. In front of Tom, on a peeling card table, lit by the thin alley of light falling through the door crack, lay the list of open jobs.

Tom called over to me. "I hear from down South it's time you got yourself a new man."

I ignored him, kept slapping body filler against the gouges in the paint.

Tom pointed to the line of men straggling through the door. "Pick yourself a new one," he said, "You got 72 hours before Jay comes back. I'll handle him."

I held up my trowel of Bondo and creme hardener. Baby pink. The sweet puke smell of body filler hit my nostrils.

"See this? I'm Bondoing myself shut. Not open for business this year." I made a motion of wiping Bondo between my legs, filling my body. Body filler. Tom laughed and waved an applicant towards the sleepers. A flabby man in worn army jungle camo shuffled towards sleeper 12.

Tom is wrong. Jay is back now, and he spent last night with me. We're a couple again; I'm sure of it. He said so. He made promises. His whispers cooled my damp breasts.

Still, I ask Al, "Do you think Jay's cheating again?"

"Oh, Sugar-booger. Why do you ask me?" Al sighs. "All I can say is this; he sat awfully close to Lou at breakfast. Mat, just leave him."

"Yeah? And go where?" I throw my beer out the cookhouse door. It clatters on the pile we keep planning to return for nickels.

Al just shrugs. I could hit him. Instead I dig my nails

into my soft wrist flesh. I'm not so excited for the new season anymore.

Under the dark blue shade of the bigtop, Tattoo Lou exercises her horses. Though Lou has tattoos all over her body, she is known for her classy training and performing. Tattoos drip from her collarbones to her ankles. Both her arms are sleeved with tattoos. Not one long continuous mural, like I've seen on Japanese gangsters in tattoo magazines. A mess of unrelated pictures brawl across her skin. The color and skill vary; different tats betray different stages in her life. Teenage rebel, biker, carny. Dealer, jail, circus.

When I was a child, around nine or ten, Lou told me she'd gotten her first tattoo with her first period. A butterfly on her breast. As she grew into a full-figured woman, the butterfly stretched and blurred. Its black outline faded to the green of tarnished copper. She told me this pointing to the ruined picture and advised me not to get tattoos till I'd stopped growing, or not to get started on them at all.

"They're addictive," she said. I didn't understand.

"I actually get high off the pain," she explained. "Just don't start."

Now, over ten years later, my skin remains marked only by scars, and she hasn't added a new tat. Lou, pushing forty, makes Tante design special costumes to cover her illustrations.

I hesitate on the entry ramp, stretching my calves against its gentle slope. My eyes slowly adjust to the bigtop twilight. Jay sits third row center ring, watching Lou flick her long whip over the horses' backs. He sits forward on the bench, elbows resting on the ringcurb.

Lou mouths, "Good, good," when her animals complete

a full turn in place. Tante said each is named for a Christian martyr. And that this is blasphemy. She crosses herself when the horses walk past the costume truck, and mutters something in Arabic. Sometimes I wonder what kind of curses Tante's God would rain down on our poor sinful heads if she didn't constantly protect us with her prayers.

After the horses complete a set of passes, Lou feeds them sweet grain from a leather bag slung low on her round hip. She scratches behind their ears. I watch Jayson watch her for a while longer before I join him ringside.

"Hey." I bump his shoulder with mine. He holds up his hand to quiet me. I slump against his body, my elbows propped next to his on the ringcurb, our outer thighs touching. His eyes remain fixed on Lou, praising her horses. Eventually she steps back and they begin trotting around the ring again, readying for another set.

The tent smells of hot horse. For a time we just sit shoulder to shoulder, thigh to thigh, watching the horses kick up ringdirt with each pass. When they don't cut their corners close enough, their hooves hit the ringcurb with a hollow thud. We sit back in the benches, leaning away from their heaving bodies, but horse sweat still sprinkles us with every pass. Lou calls them to the center with a small gesture and a faint word; they line up obediently. After a long wide curve through the air, her whip cracks across their shoulders. They bow to her. I wonder if any of this hurts.

"New act," Jay says.

"Looks just like last year's," I say.

"It's totally different," he says, curling his lip and shaking his head slightly. "It's gonna open the second half, Fabrizio decided."

Now the horses prance sideways, crossing one leg in front of the other. Lou motions, and they turn counterclockwise, bodies close. I can barely see her lips move when she gives directions. With the subtlest gesture, the softest whisper, Lou commands the powerful animals. The middle horse, a beautiful white gelding, peels off the line and begins a slow march around the ring. The rest follow in order, each making a 360-degree turn in place when they get back to their original position. Only the graceful white holds my attention. Just like only Lou holds Jay's.

I say, "I can't believe people pay to watch horses walk around. Only the white one's worth watching." The white bears his neck higher; his eyes focus on the last row. I bet he's thinking of places bigger than the ring.

"What do you think of her?" Jay asks.

"What do you mean?"

"I mean, what do you think of her?" he says, with the emphasis on "think" and "her," as if that clears things up.

"I think she's . . . " I stop to think. "I don't know what you want me to say. Lou's been around so long she's about as exciting to me as the pump-out man." I don't ask, Why the sudden interest? I remember Tom laughing.

"I think she really understands those horses." Jay's eyes narrow as if he's squinting into a great light. My eyes follow his into the ring, and I look for whatever he sees. All I see is horses rearing on their hind legs and balancing unnaturally while Lou twirls the whip in wide slow circles across their breastbones.

"She's in complete control," he says.

"She should be; she's been doing the same goddamn act since I was four."

"Has not. It's totally different."

"Well then, what do you want me to say? Why'd you even ask?"

Jay leans forward and places his hands on the ringcurb,

his elbows locked rigid. He's wearing a muscle tee, and his tan triceps flex under a veil of soft dark hair. "We've been talking a lot lately. You know, in Sarasota, before her act, you know. . . ."

"I've heard."

"It's not like that. She's been through a lot."

I look at this man I have slept with for over six years, and wonder what "been through a lot" means.

"You know what people are saying, Jay," I warn.

"Fuck 'em. It's not like that. Fuck 'em." He runs his hand lightly down my thigh. "When are you gonna start trusting me again, Babe?" His palm cups my knee, but his eyes stay on Lou. I can't answer, because I don't know.

Horse practice is over. Lou throws blankets on the horses' backs. She leads them through the chute and out into the cold morning. The white follows last, slow, cool. I wish I could ride him down the cracked runway to the beach at the ancient empty Coast Guard station. We could gallop without a saddle, without whips, without sweet corn to bribe, my arms wrapped around his neck, my chest flat out on his back. One unit. Nothing extra between our bodies. That's how people and horses should be, I think.

Jay pushes to his feet and steps over the ringcurb. Without another word, he begins raking the ringdirt. After a while there is nothing for me to do but leave.

I run into Tom on my way to the cookhouse for a second cup of coffee. We walk across the old runway slowly. I kick up tufts of winter-burned seagrass drying in the runway cracks.

He says, "New crew looks good. They seem ready to go. I'm ready to go. You ready to go?"

We throw our bodies against the hangar door. Stiff

wheels slide along rusty tracks. Turning sideways, we scrape through the rib-squeezing crack into the dank gray hangar. The massive door slams. It cuts out the day. Wind off the bay rattles the windows, loose in their dried caulk beds.

"I'm always ready to go," I answer. "Tent ready?"

"Near. We got to mount a prop for Lou. Disco ball, center of the cupola. You got to deal with it. I'd do it, but you know." He holds up his left hand, juts his chin to indicate the space where his three main fingers used to be.

"Sure," I say. He nods and wanders over to the sleepers. I head towards the cookhouse; Tom slaps sleeper doors with his lobster-claw hand, yelling, "Wake up, you good-for-nothing lazy-ass New-Jack First-of-May motherfuckers!" New crew tumble out their sleepers.

Lou isn't in the horse tent like I thought she'd be. Her assistant, a small dark nameless boy, brushes down the horses. He doesn't speak, not to me or anyone. We don't know if it's because he doesn't know English or because he's shy. He's definitely not deaf; Tante tested by sneaking behind him and shouting in his ear. He near jumped out his skin. He's not stupid either; he's good with horses and disappears every time someone in a uniform comes near the lot. We call him the Counselor as a joke. Rumor is he's been stealing women's panties from the shower truck and wearing them under his overalls.

I show the Counselor sugar cubes cradled in my hand. He nods. The white gelding stands quietly in his stall. He follows me with his eyes. Approaching slowly, I let him catch my smell before I'm in kicking range. He bows his head a bit. I slide forward, leading with the sugar in my outstretched palm. His nose bends to my hand. His soft lips feel like a wet velvet kiss against my skin.

"Good, good," I say, and pat my damp hand against the muscular round of his cheek. The solid clap satisfies me, and I could stand with him a good long time, maybe lean against the strong wall of his shoulder, his flank. On tiptoe, I circle my arms around his neck and brush my lips against his jaw. He lets me. I lean into his soft, clean hide. When the Counselor finally wakes me with a cough, I back out of the stall, embarrassed.

My knock rattles Lou's screen door, crooked in the frame. She hasn't blocked her trailer level, though she's been up nearly two days from Sarasota now. From the outside, Lou's trailer smells like manure just spread. She should've pumped out in Florida. The pump-out man won't come to this old airfield. Says it's off his route. Our winter Porta-John filled up by January, so we squatted outside. I wonder why she doesn't just shit outside like the rest of us. Maybe her performer butt is too delicate for the cold air blowing off the bay.

"Hey there," she says. Lou speaks with a vague accent. There's a rhythm and roundness to her words. When I was younger, I would practice pushing my mouth into strange shapes, forcing my flat vowels to match her rich ones. I thought she was glamorous. Even now, whenever I speak with her, my voice creeps towards her accent, borrowing pronunciations and phrases from her, against my will.

"Hey there," I answer.

I peek through the musty screen. She lies on her bed, half covered with a sheet, wearing the smallest lace-up black leather vest a woman of her size can pull around herself. Her colorful breasts burst over the top, perfectly round. I step in, leaving the door open behind me, hoping the foul air will escape.

Lou stretches out one leg and toes the door shut, trapping the manure smell in. The sheet shifts, and I catch a glimpse of continuous color up her solid thigh, hip, the dip at her waist, unbroken by any fabric. Then she readjusts the sheet; covered again.

"Tom told me you need a prop mounted?" I say, leaning against the sink. It's full of gray water; bits of lettuce and a few hairs float on top.

"Yeah, it's somewhere in the back closet. I'll get it." She raises up on her elbows, and her breasts crush together. A soldier dives into the deep crack; a stone tower split by lightning tumbles into the dark crevice. I imagine running my hand between her breasts and rescuing these fallen illustrations.

"No, I'll get it," I say, turning towards the closet.

It's a heavy globe, the surface bumpy with silver squares. On top is a small motor that will turn it. I hold it carefully, frightened by its weight and value.

"Wait. Before you go, could you fix my sink?" she calls. I'm halfway down her crooked aluminum stairs. I tuck the ball behind her rear wheel and come back in.

"It's clogged," she says. "I don't know anything about plumbing, or I'd do it myself."

"You tried a plunger?"

"Yeah. Could you maybe just stick a hanger down it or something? I'm scared I'll mess it up myself."

I straighten a hanger into a snake and fish through the stinking water to the clogged drain. My knuckles graze the soft thick water. My stomach lurches.

But she's at my side with a beer. With achy head and uneasy stomach, I figure, why not? I swallow a mouthful of the warm sour Blatz. The fake St. Pauli girl beams at me from the can. She's a brunette, and she's on beer brewed in Brooklyn. She's a failure.

Lou stands close to me, naked from the bottom of her tiny vest to her red toenails. I look down at the swirling water draining slowly instead of the snake wrapped around her thigh, the orchid that grows from her public hair.

"I remember when you were a little girl." She lifts a hank of my hair off my shoulder, as if testing its weight. "Now you're old enough to drink beer and unclog my drain." The sink gurgles.

Lou knew my mother. I have faint memories of them trading magazines, sunning in lawn chairs, fixing each other's hair. They are close in age; they were best friends. When I was little, Lou tied ribbons around my ponytails and taught me to style and curtsy; soft elbows, pretty hands. After Ma ran off, I followed Lou around, begging for an explanation, attention, anything. She always waved me off, said Ma never said shit about leaving. Exactly like that. "Never said shit about leaving. Just up and went." Mostly Lou ignored me. Eventually I stopped hanging around.

A big silence hangs in the air, too long for my comfort; I concentrate on swallowing enough of the warm Blatz so I can leave.

She throws herself down across her unmade bed and says, "Mind if I get high?"

"Sure, why not?" I think maybe she'll give me a hit, and that it's been a while since I've seen pot. Drugs are hard to come by in winter quarters; we're too isolated. Good weed is worth hanging around and choking back a warm beer.

I feel a vague anticipatory glow, till I see her tie off her biceps with a length of black marline. Casual, like she's making tea for a guest, she cooks her shit up in a spoon over a candle. She drops cotton in the spoon's well, soaking up the liquid, and pierces it with a needle. She pulls out the plunger and draws it into the syringe, then taps it a few times and squirts a minuscule drop over the tip like I've seen doctors do. She shoots. After she releases the tieline, I ask why she tapped the syringe and squirted some over the tip. I always wondered why doctors do that. Seems like a waste. She lays her needle down and relaxes onto the bed.

"Air bubbles. If you get a big one in your vein, it can blow out your heart, or brain, I can't remember which," she says.

"You ever seen that happen?" I pour the rest of my beer down the sink. The drain works fine now, but a thin ring of brown foam marks the old waterline. "Maybe it can't."

She shakes her head. I can see her movements getting slower, like she's under water or far away. I wonder if Ma ever shot up with her.

"It's not such a big deal. I knew this guy who would shoot up an air bubble and push it around his vein. He did it on purpose, but he didn't untie until he sucked it back out with the syringe. He was in complete control."

I pick up the syringe and hold the needle close to my face. It seems too small for the job.

"You have total control with that thing," she continues. "My old man taught me to pierce the vein, then suck the blood back into the spike and shoot that mix back in, back and forth a couple or five times, 'cause that's how you made a hit. You know, a vein. You gotta not come out the other side."

I lay the syringe carefully on the windowsill. I don't look at the bright sunlight shining through the clear plastic body. I don't want to know if I really saw a faint pink tinge, or if that was just my imagination. She's full of shit, I figure. Talking out her ass. I wish she'd put on more clothes. Her hand rests lightly on her breast, cupping the fallen tower fondly. My mind, unasked, places Jayson's hand there. I wonder if he mixes his blood in the syringe, plays with air bubbles.

Her eyes have closed. A fly lands on the spoon, then flies to the counter. I watch it walk over what looks like dried eggs on a green plastic plate. The trailer smells sweet and close, of unwashed dishes and an overfull holding tank. I want to open a window, but it's not my place. The fly twitches across the plate. Eventually Lou opens her eyes, and I ask her how she feels.

Eyes shut again, she says, "Like I'm drinking hot chocolate in front of a warm fire. And it's Christmas." She smiles. "Like coming home."

And I want to be there with her so badly.

It feels later than eight P.M. Dinner began an hour ago, but we're not eating with the others. Noise drifts from the cookhouse; laughter, forks hitting plates.

When he arrived from Sarasota, in convoy with Lou, Jay parked his trailer outside the hangar but separate from the performers' trailer circle behind the tent. Separate from the crew, separate from the performers. He believes bosses should remain a mystery. For discipline purposes. So far his new ringcrew has only heard him speak at rehearsals, giving orders or cursing their stupidity.

Jay sits on a folding chair inside his trailer, facing the screen door. We dosed behind the tent during rehearsal intermission, did the second half tripping. No big deal; the show barely changes. Dogs, fliers, clown entrées, elephants, tumblers, jugglers, and of course horses. I open and close the back-door flap, Jay pushes props around the ring. Different performers, same acts. Or in Lou's case, same performer, new act. But it's really all the same year in, year out. The cues are like breathing or shitting or sex, we've done so many shows. New props, new costumes, no change.

Though he's just returned from a five week absence, Jay already feels like a habit again. Like he never left, like we've been staring at the door forever, not just four minutes. But that's all it's been; I looked at my watch before, and just now.

"Did you ever notice," he says to me, "how you can only either focus on the screen of the door or what lies beyond the screen? You can't see both clearly at once."

I focus on the screen, then on empty gray expanse beyond it. A thin acacia bends low to a cracked cement blockade. It's amazing how these trees grow out of any small crack, clinging to the smallest patch of soil. Far away, red and white lights twinkle; somewhere across the bay, people live in neat white houses. A plane roars overhead, past this abandoned strip to the modern airport two miles away. Gulls drop clams on the hangar roofs and swoop to pick meat from the broken shells.

I try to see both the screen and the outside clearly, but can't. I try crossing my eyes, then I put my hand over my right eye and remove it quickly.

"That won't work," he says about my eye trick. "I tried it already. The key is to control your focus. If I can control my focus enough to see both the screen in the door and the scene beyond the door, then I will be between dimensions. That's what I'm working on. It's a trip."

His eyes don't fix on any one point. They rove around the room, dry and twitching.

"Lou showed me these books. You know, Indians use mushrooms to get visions." His hands play bongo on my head, he speaks in rhythm. "Rastas smoke ganga to hang with Jah. That's what it's all about." Hands drop, serious now. "If I do it right, I can break down all my old constructs and move past all this. Pierce the veil, Babe. I'm crossing over."

"I'll believe it when I see it. You sure we're taking the same shit?" I try to laugh when I say this, but my throat is too tight and I only manage a strangled cough.

"That's the problem with your generation, Mat. You just don't understand. It's not about getting high. It's about changing your whole personality."

I wonder, if he changes his personality, what will happen to me? Where would that leave me? I would ask him, but he's far away, floating beyond my reach. Trying to cross over, I guess.

He works on this while I smoke a cigarette. If I smoke steadily, it takes me seven minutes to finish a Lucky. Tante timed me once. When I'm done, I leave.

Al sits in a lawn chair out front of our sleeper. He wears black silk pajama bottoms and a short red kimono. I stare at the drink balanced on Al's knee for a moment before he redirects my attention to an empty lawn chair by scraping its metal legs against the poured cement floor. This is possibly the worst sound I've ever heard. Shoulders around my ears, I lower myself onto the frayed plastic webbing.

"Sorry, Al, sorry, sorry, sorry," I mumble at his scolding finger.

"You're stoned." Al pours me a drink from the metal pitcher at his feet. My hand aims itself towards the glass.

My eyes fix stubbornly on a workbench littered with files and grinders. Iron shavings glitter under overbright hangar lights. Yet inches from the bench, a pile of rags shifts in the shadows. I shudder involuntarily.

"What are you doing, dosing at rehearsals?" With the

drink and a long-ashed Virginia Slim in his hand, he looks like the jilted lover in a black and white movie.

"What? Why you giving me shit all the time, Al? He just got back. We're hanging out again is all. He was gone five weeks." I hold up my fingers to illustrate.

Al pokes me in the shoulder with a bony finger. "You'd better straighten out is all, Girlfriend."

My fingers hang suspended in a peace sign. I can't remember what Al is talking about. Besides, my drink is empty.

"Hey, what is this stuff?" I hold my glass up to the light coming out our sleeper door. There appears to be a worm in my drink. I look again, and it becomes a green twig.

"Pimm's and ginger with mint. Very classy."

Classy. Tattoo Lou dances across the inside of my forehead.

"Hey, what do you think of Lou?" I ask Al.

Al crosses his legs and sips his cocktail. "That freak show? She's a bit overdone. I mean, a delicate rose on a well-groomed buttock is attractive, but she is bum nasty. Old too. Ink on skin does not age well."

"Yeah, but what do you think of her? I mean, do you think she's been through a lot?"

"Been through a lot? What the hell does that mean? Child, she's as deep as my pores." Al refills my glass. I hadn't noticed it was empty.

"You're jealous." I raise my glass in cheers.

"Please, of that poor white trash?"

"Tante says she's rich."

"Yeah, and I heard she has royal blood, like she's a duchess or countess or some such British thing." He raises his glass to mine.

"Bullshit, Al. She's Australian."

"Girlfriend, that ain't no Australian accent."

"Well, I heard it from Giselle," I say.

"And I heard from Tante that Lou was a debutante."

"Well, then she can't be a foreigner." There.

Al stops with his mouth open. I reach over and shut it for him.

He says, "You're right. That accent must be fake, like Tina Turner's. But I think Tina earned hers, don't you?"

I sip my drink and try to remember something about Tina Turner.

Delicately, Al fishes the green twig out of his drink and sucks it clean. Then he drops it back in and says, "Come to think of it, I heard from Tante that Lou got herself all mixed up with Colombians. Coke and guns and whatnot. Way back, before you was a twinkle in your daddy's pants. She was disowned for going south with some swarthy man after her coming out. Isn't that too much? It certainly isn't a party girl's world anymore." Al snaps his fingers in front of my slack face.

"Coke? I thought she was a junkie." I try to suck delicately on my green twig. A little piece gets caught in my teeth and I drop the rest to the ground trying to pick it out.

"Oh, please. Miss Thing is a garbagehead. She'll do anything to get off." Al crosses his legs at the ankle and fixes his kimono. After a while he sighs. "I wish some swarthy man would take me to South America. I mean, God, it's been ages since I've seen anything beyond trailers and Porta-Johns." He waves his hand weakly around the hangar.

"You are jealous."

He pretends not to hear. "I'd settle for a quick trip to Paris. Actually, I'd settle for anywhere with a decent espresso."

"Don't be so dramatic, Al. You've just been in this

hangar too long. I'll take you to Paris someday. Or at least out to coffee."

"Espresso, dear. Besides, there's something definitely lacking in your—how shall we say?—nether region?" Al points to his crotch with his twig.

My jaw feels tight, and I realize I am grinding my teeth. I hope another drink will take the edge off.

"Why the sudden interest in the tattoo beast? She's as old as Death and been here since the Dark Ages." Al sounds like he's talking through a long cardboard tube.

"Jay suddenly thinks she's been through a lot." Didn't I already explain this?

"Oh, Jay thinks so. What did I tell you this morning about your man? If you aren't gonna leave him, it's time for a tighter rein. What are you doing here getting drunk with me? I think you should go find that man of yours before he and Lou go through a lot together."

"He says it's not like that. He promised this time."

"Please," Al says.

It's after midnight. I guess this based on the fact that Tom has already turned off the generator truck to save on diesel. The only lights on the lot are the performers' and bosses'; they hook up to private gennies.

I cradle the reassuring weight of a quart of Jack in my arms. Voices drift from Jay's Tioga, one female. Briefly I consider turning back to my sleeper and drinking the bottle myself. Or sharing it with Al. Instead I stand outside and listen. After a few moments I twist the bottle cap. The paper seal tears cleanly; the bourbon warms my throat, chest, stomach.

I still can't understand what is said, so I lean my ear against the aluminum to hear better. The trailer tips slightly against my cheek with someone's shift of weight. I consider standing there all night, sensing their movements through small shifts of the trailer, and then wonder what is wrong with me. When I drink again, I'm surprised at the level of the brown liquor. It's now an inch below the neck. This level must be deceiving, an illusion created by the narrow neck. It can't possibly hold a lot because it's so narrow, so I really didn't drink so much after all. Close the bottle; go in without knocking. After all, I practically live here.

Lou sits on Jay's pull-out bed with her shirt pulled up and tucked under her chin. Her finger hovers over a distorted tattoo on her long left breast. A skull flanked by wings. They turn their smiling faces towards me.

"Hey, Baby." Jay stands like he'd been expecting me. The inside of his elbow hooks around the nape of my neck; he pulls me into the room and kisses my forehead.

"Hey, look, it's Matty. Hey, Matty, Lou came over 'cause she's pretty nervous about the new act, you know? She wanted to go over a few things before tomorrow's dress." His voice slurs softly. He speaks easily, artificially relaxed. The musky sage smell of pot hangs in the curtains.

"Hey, Baby." Lou smiles at me.

"Hey." I stand stiffly against Jay's body, the bottle gripped in my hand. I shake it slightly, sending the liquor into waves.

"Whad'ya have there?" Lou asks, as if she isn't half naked in Jay's trailer. Beneath her left breast grows a lovely forest, the enchanted kind with toadstools and fairy rings. Under her right, a stormy sea. A dragon flying over the waves reaches for the gold hoops that hang from her hard pink nipples. I could get lost in the worlds illustrated on her torso.

"Jack." I hand her the bottle. She swallows and passes it to Jay. Leaning against the sink, I fight the urge to pull Lou's shirt down. She's forgotten all about it, and though she released her chin grip to drink, the shirt remains half raised, caught by tension across her breasts.

"Well, looks like we got ourselves a party." Jay raises the bottle in cheers and drinks.

"Sit, sit." He pats a tight space between him and Lou. "My two favorite ladies," he continues, like the good host. I sit next to Jay, my hip pressed against his. It tingles where we touch.

He hugs us both around the waist. I don't know what to say, or what to feel. My skin is tight, electric. As if I've been turned inside out and all my nerve endings lie exposed and naked. I drink and pass Jay the bottle. His fingers find the sensitive spot where my overalls button at my hipbone. When Lou places the bottle back in my hands, her fingertips graze my knuckles and rest there for a moment.

The bottle goes round again. Then Jay slaps his knee. "I know what we need!" Laying a hand on my thigh and a hand on Lou's, he presses himself up.

"Too hot," Lou mumbles. She pulls her shirt over her head and flings it towards the kitchenette. I avoid the sharks swimming around her biceps by concentrating on the noises Jay makes in the bathroom. A crash.

"Shit. Fuck. Oh yes . . . "

He returns with two candles, a red one in a clear glass tube printed with a prayer to St. Jude, and a black skull-shaped one. He lights these with stove matches, then turns to us smiling, hands spread.

"Hey, like that?" He gestures around the trailer as if everything has changed.

"Mmm." This from Lou. Then she reaches for me and licks my ear with her very wet tongue. I jerk my head out of her hand. She laughs; I finish the bottle.

"Wait, I got a joint in here somewhere." She grabs her shoulder bag off the table and dumps the contents on the bed: a hairbrush, a tampon, a syringe, a bag of white powder, a glass vial and a box of straight razors, a pack of Marlboros, a green plastic lighter. No wallet. Once she'd told me her dead body could be identified by her tats, even decapitated. So she never carries ID.

Lou reaches for the Marlboros twice before her fingers close around the pack. Holding the box close to her eyes, she pulls out a thin joint. Jayson joins us on the bed with matches. I think I've got to catch up.

We pass the joint like the Jack before. Then Jay slaps his forehead with his hand. He sways to the kitchenette. The open refrigerator releases a wave of sour cold air. I swallow hard. Jay returns with a forty of Old E. After I smoke one of Lou's cigarettes, I feel better.

The beer goes; I barely notice it make the rounds. Outside, the sky is orange like those marshmallow candies called Circus Peanuts. I comment on the color, and Lou says, "Light pollution." Jay looks as if he's proved an important point.

My abdomen is tight against my jeans. "Gotta pee."

"Go outside, tank's full," Jay says. "Fuckin' pump-out man is MIA."

Lou laughs and waves. She falls back on the bed.

Cold wind screams off the abandoned Coast Guard beach. It rattles the windows in the hangar door, snaps sidewall lines against sidepoles with sharp metal pings, slaps the horse tent flaps against each other in startling claps. The horses stamp and chuff. I head through the thick senseless sounds towards the horses. Something hits my shin hard, and I look down at the white painted head on a stake. How did I get so close already?

"Fuckit." This to the white gelding. Here he is, my old friend. Mind if I? I squat there, in his horse-warm stall. The hay tickles my butt. I hover unsteadily, then rest my hand on his hard thigh for balance. He snorts, but stands steady.

When I'm done, I lean against his flank and smoke a Lucky. For seven minutes I consider going back to my sleeper.

"I really should," I tell the horse. He flicks his tail against my shoulder.

Knowing what Jay probably wants, I weigh that possibility against leaving the two of them alone. I tell the gelding, "No, I'm definitely going home." But we both know I'm lying.

Lou gyrates slowly to the Stones. She moans "Angie" into her hairbrush microphone, giving the name more syllables than Mick does. Jayson lies across his bed, legs propped on the sink, singing into a Bud longneck.

"Hey, Babe." He pulls me onto the bed and opens my lips with his tongue. I sink into this familiar taste of tobacco and beer. There's still a hint of pot at the back of his mouth. I enjoy this too. He lifts my shirt with his beer; the glass is cold and wet against my skin. When I feel his calluses on my breasts, I relax my shoulders. I wish Lou would leave so I could sleep. Fingers curled into his gray hairs, I put my cheek on Jay's chest and close my eyes.

"Hey now, hey. None of that; no sleeping on the party." Jay jerks me into a sitting position.

"Oh man," I mumble. Lou changes the tape; I figure a cigarette will wake me up. The smell of burnt hair hits my nostrils, and I realize I'm leaning on the hand that holds my cigarette. I don't remember lighting it. When I put my fingertips on Jay's table to steady things, the wood grain flows past them like water.

Lou dances over with the plastic cassette box in her hand. Jefferson Airplane. Grace Slick moans, "One pill makes you smaller . . . "

"You know, this song is deep. I mean, have you ever listened to the lyrics? It's about *Alice in Wonderland*," Lou says. "Fuckin' Alice in Wonderfuckingland." Lou sits between Jay and me, shifting her ass around like she's digging a hole between us.

"This is old," I say to Jayson, who is nodding like he's never heard this tape that he's owned for over a decade.

"Yeah, but do you really get what it's about?" Jay says.

"Who doesn't at this point?" I say. No reaction. It would be better all around if I do the dishes, I decide.

The faucet coughs a few times before tepid water dribbles out. No dish soap on the counter or under the sink. Finally I go to the bathroom for a bar of Ivory. The lame stream of water barely makes bubbles when I rub the soap bar against a pink plastic Scrubbee. Halfway through the pile, I need a drink. Over the sink I find a bottle of vermouth. Red and sweet. Jay and Lou move from *Alice in Wonderland* to *The Wizard of Oz*. Lou says something about the scene where Dorothy and her friends fall asleep in the poppies and its meaning in relation to the monkeys that land on their backs later in the movie. Her voice holds the wonder-filled tone of little kids telling store Santas what they want for Christmas.

I figure it's got to be around 3 by now. Somehow the dishes are done. I tell the dishes drying on the rack, "I could go home," but they don't respond, and neither do Jay and Lou. Instead Jay mentions he's out of acid, and Lou nods like this has something to do with what she just said. They both seem so terribly far away that I figure I'll never make it from the sink to the bed. But I'm there between them, and Lou's shoulder feels a lot like Ma's way back when. I could almost sleep. Or cry. Lou's voice rumbles through her soft body. It says the song about a horse of a different color in Emerald City is about heroin. "You know. Horse? Heroin?"

While Lou taps powder out of the small glass jar, I remember the needle and realize I can't go through with this. "I can't do this," I tell Lou, gesturing towards the syringe.

"Sure you can, Honey. We aren't shooting. Can't have dope dick, now can we?" She laughs and swats Jay. "Get this out of here," she commands, and he sweeps her works into her bag.

"We're sniffing, Baby," she coos. Her voice is Borden's condensed milk in a can, thick and sweet.

She chops the powder with a straight razor, reordering it in neat piles, then lines. As she chops, she talks. She sounds like she's telling a bedtime story; her words singsong rhythmically with her razor taps.

"Every time I do cocaine, I want to get fucked in the ass. There was this Mexican bear trainer, I mean a Mexican who trained bears, not Mexican bears, maybe he wasn't Mexican, doesn't matter."

She snorts two lines through a rolled dollar bill, then hands it to Jay. A string of mucus hangs between her nostril and the bill tube; Jay carries it to his nose. When he's sniffed the remaining two, she runs a wet finger over the table and rubs it against her gums.

"Anyhow, he had this pink cocaine, I swear it was pink. Pink!" Lou picks a bit of powder out of the jar with a tiny spoon and holds it to my face, cupping one hand underneath, like a mother spooning soup to a sick child. I sniff obediently.

She serves my other nostril, asking, "This your first time?"

I nod, tilting my head to prevent snot from running out my burning nose.

She cuts more lines. "And we did it and then he fucked me in the ass."

She chops and sniffs. She chops, Jay sniffs. She chops and hands me the dollar tube, like I'm a big girl now, I can feed myself now.

"You wanna fuck me?"

I don't know who she's asking. She unhooks my overall straps.

"Mat—you gotta cock, Mat? You want to watch Jay fuck me? He's got a cock. Show us your cock, Jay."

The trailer smells hot and close, like sweat. We lie on the bed naked, bodies close, Jay between us. I can barely see Lou's lips move as she gives directions. Movement is slow and confused. There are many arms and legs; I keep losing track of my own. Lou motions and Jay turns me 180 degrees towards her. I become distracted by the fish swimming through her ribcage, the eagles nesting on her hip. Her hands make wide slow circles across my breasts.

Curious, clinical, I explore her. So this is how it looks, I think as I examine a pierce, a tattoo, her vagina. I note the smell—like sheets after sex, the taste—lemon and salt, texture—like an oyster. I remember the biology book a bleacher boy showed me long ago. The pictures of the segmented worm, the frog, the man and woman. Illustrated onionskin pages peeled away to reveal layers of internal organs underneath. I decide her vagina looks more like a dried pear half than an oyster.

When Jay enters Lou, I expect to be jealous, but I'm nothing. I look at this man I have fucked for over six years and wonder what this means. Then I wonder if I'm still high, but I lose that thought tracing the horses galloping across Lou's heaving back. When Jay pushes her off to finish in me, I focus on the screen door, and what lies beyond it.

In me, he says, "Tell Lou how you like it."

I don't understand till he raises his hand over me.

"Hard." I mouth the word.

"Louder." He pulls his hand back farther. There is a familiar tension in his fist.

"Hard, *I like it hard!*" I scream at them both.

"Good, good," Lou says.

Only now do I return to my body, ashamed.

Horse dress rehearsal. I limp across the ancient run-ways to the bigtop. Too bright morning. The sun burns through my skin to my bruised and dirty parts inside.

Bitter coke-stained mucus drips down the back of my throat, and I remember last night. I can look down on my body like looking down on a black and white photo. Jay's behind me; she's in front. I'm pinned in the middle.

Hush now, they murmur. Relax and it won't hurt so much.

They fight inside me, tearing through the thin membrane wall. They hurt me. She enjoys it, he does.

I do too.

My abdomen cramps. Sharp and swift like a cut. I kneel on the pocked tarmac, clutching my stomach. I bite the

insides of my cheeks, my tongue, I bang my head with my
fists.

My rigging knife presses into my left thigh. I could use it
to peel off every inch of skin that enjoyed being touched
last night. I could stick it up me, gut myself like a fish.
Maybe, if I'm raw hollowed-out meat, I'll feel clean again.

Broken clamshells and pebbles mark my face. I'm
curled on the tarmac in a fetal position. I'm going crazy. No
one can find out I'm crazy. I tell myself over and over: I can
control this. I can.

The ringside seats are actually quite full. Performers
take up most of the center section; Ringmaster Fabrizio sits
alone in a box seat. Tante hovers near the chute, hidden in
the shadows of side grandstand.

Electricians perch ready on their spot platforms; the
band tunes up on the bandstand. Jayson doesn't sit; he
stands stiffly at the curtain, ready to pull it open. I feel like
I'm the only one uninterested in this new act, this new
opening for the second half. The tent looks alien to me; if Al
didn't have me by my elbow, I'd run from this blue canvas
cage. Instead we join Tom ringside.

The music begins, one long high note. In the middle of
the gold velour curtain a white stain of light widens. The
other instruments join in. Someone hidden lowers the mirrored ball from the rigging.

"Goddamn ball," Tom whispers. Side spots hit the rotating mirrors with cool colored gels. Sharp flashes of blue
and purple scatter around the tent. An appreciative murmur rises from the center section; all the performers wish
their lighting was so dramatic. Blue and purple shards stab
my swollen brain. Even with both hands secured around

my mug, I can't raise the coffee to my lips; when I try, I shake so hard it spills over.

The music throbs in rhythm with my head, and I wonder how I'll get through this act. This day, this life.

In the ring, the curtains open slowly to reveal the white gelding. Lou steps into the ring wearing white sequined gauze. A spot picks her up, sends pink shimmers rippling through the tent. Her costume covers every tattoo, yet she doesn't look frumpy, just classy.

"Tante's outdone herself," Tom says.

"Yeah, she's got a good eye for detail." I wonder if Tom can smell last night on me.

Lou hits the gelding on his flank, sending him center ring, into a blinding white spot. Two gauze wings sprout from his shoulders. Covered with mirrors, they flash as brilliantly as the disco ball. Purple and blue sparks bounce off the wings as the horse shies sideways, out of the spot. He's not used to the wings' weight; or maybe the bright new lighting spooks him.

Lou's whip flicks. She hisses. The gelding freezes, and the spot catches him again. Now Lou steps regally into the ring and holds him under the light by his bridle. She styles, bows; we clap on cue.

Jay steps from the wings to receive her cape. With a flourish, she whips it off and over the gelding's head. He paws the dirt. He blows air hard through his nostrils.

She mumbles, "Good, good." Calming. Warning.

Jay folds her cape over his arm, bows slightly to her. She styles again; we clap again.

The music changes to an upbeat version of "Eight Miles High." I want to hold my hands over my ears, but I can't figure out where to put my coffee mug.

Music booming; lights flashing; the tent's heating up. I look for signs of special communication between Lou and Jay. But she concentrates on putting the white gelding through a round of solo tricks. After one chorus, Jay opens the curtain again, to let in four more horses.

These only wear headdresses of white feathers. Lou cracks her whip and they all 360 in line. The winged gelding spins in the middle. Halfway through this spin, his wings hit the eyes of the gray to his left. Tom flinches. Jay half steps toward the ring. Tante disappears under the sidewall. I drop my coffee between the floorboards.

Lou's lips move fast now, but the music carries away her commands. The frightened gray ignores her. He bites the white's wings. Her whip flicks the gray. She aims for the white. Instead of grazing his flank, her whip catches his costume.

The wings shift forward, tumble in his face.

A deep intake of collective breath.

The white gelding takes off around the ring. He runs full tilt, tries to shake off the wings. His hooves pound the ringcurb. Silently, I cheer him on.

Lou whips, shouts. He doesn't hear. He is running from those stupid wings, this stupid act. He shakes his head wildly. Feathers and sequins fly off his back. The other horses shy from his heaving costume. We sit frozen in our seats, watching Lou lose control.

The horse aims to break out. Runs for the chute, the gold curtain. The other horses step aside, give him plenty of room for escape. But Jay steps in front of the velour, blocking this exit.

He gallops past Jay. Vaults over the ringcurb and out the ring. Ringmaster Fabrizio yells Italian to Tom; Tom looks at me. The white gelding heads for the sidewall.

Tom and I run behind him now. We're afraid for the tent. Stopped short by the blue vinyl, the horse banks hard left, escapes under side grandstand.

Tom and I follow him into the steel maze that supports the seats.

Under the bleachers it's dark and close, the only light a small amount of sun filtering through gaps and pinholes in the sidewall. Blue steel beams cross in confusion, supporting floorboards and seats. Garbage nets hung between the steel stringers hold fragrant reminders of last year's season. Panicked feet thud above us.

Ahead, the horse trots around the outer ring of scaffolding. The enclosed space must frustrate him; every jerk of his head kicks a floorboard out of place. Each board knocked out reveals a rectangle of show lights; purple and blue lights escape the ring and shine down through the holes. Bright colors dance across the steel structure.

"We have to get him before he knocks the whole thing down on our heads," Tom says quietly. The horse whinnies and kicks a stringer support. The bleachers groan.

Tom yells up through a knocked-out floorboard hole. "Get off the bleachers, you damn fools. If he knocks out a stringer, the whole thing'll collapse." The feet and voices move away.

We creep forward carefully. Like walking the high wire, our hands held out in front. For blindness, balance, warning, protection. I have difficulty picking through the confused darkness of this usually familiar terrain. The smell of rotted cotton candy and mildewed net mixes with horse sweat and horse fear.

"I found him," I yell. Tom appears at my shoulder.

Actually, I heard him breathing before I saw him. He lies in a tangled heap of gauze and mirrors. His wings are wrapped around the main support of center section G, his head caught in a garbage net. His left hind leg bends at an unnatural angle, while the rest of his heaving body is wedged between the boards of the hippodrome track and the muddy ground.

"Stay and watch him," Tom says.

"He isn't going anywhere," I say, but Tom has already ducked under the sidewall.

Heat rises off the horse's steaming hide. He can't move, pinned as he is. I crouch closer to him, butt to heels. I look in his eyes and not at those wings. His eyes are rolled back and up, so he can see me even though he can't turn his head.

"Hey now, hey. Don't be afraid," I say. "Relax and it won't hurt so much." I consider touching him, but worry that might spook him. Above our heads, people argue about what went wrong. Lou's voice filters down, blaming. The horse and I look at each other. There is talk of missed cues, foolish costuming, unrealistic expectations.

"How do you feel?" I ask the horse this only to hear my voice, as if by talking to him I do something worthwhile. He stares at me, not moving.

"Do you hurt much?" I know he does. "Don't be afraid. It's gonna be okay. Lie still; it'll all be over soon." I hear Tom above us now, telling Lou the situation. She tells him to go ahead, just give her a chance to get the other horses out the tent.

His breathing slows. I tell him Tom will fix him up fine. That it wasn't his fault. The act was stupid, and it wasn't fair to spring those dumb wings on him like that. It's not like he had a choice. It's not like he could've gone home.

There's a flash of light. Tom ducks under the sidewall. My knees crack when I straighten up.

Tom also tells the horse it's going to be okay. "Good, good," we both murmur, like parents to a sick child. The horse doesn't struggle anymore. He's simply looking up at me, waiting till this is all over.

Tom moves me back with gentle pressure on my arm. But I watch when he raises the rifle to his shoulder. I watch Tom aim, inches from the pure white head.

I tell my future self to remember this always: The white day bleeding under the dark blue sidewall, the horse's ragged breath, Tom's smell of tobacco and diesel, the cold bead of perspiration tracking from my armpit to my waist. How the horse's eyes are wet. How they shine. How they hold mine.

Wide open, I look and listen. The moment when the trigger sticks before it engages. Last swallow, last blink. The last breath in, no chance for out. I'm looking and listening when Tom drops him. The horse shudders once, and is still.

I crouch near the horse again, butt to heels. His eyes are in the same position, rolled back and up, but the light doesn't reflect in them so well anymore. Already he has death cataracts. The hole in the middle of his forehead releases the sweet milk smell of bone and blood suddenly exposed. A fly lands on the bullet hole. It walks jerkily around the edge, tasting.

Tom rests his hand on my shoulder. "How do you feel?"

"Fine," I say, but I don't move. What I'm thinking is this: I've never seen the exact moment of death so close. I've seen already dead; I've seen the process of dying, but never the transition. Never the death.

I say, "It's just interesting, you know? Like in a scientific way. Like biology."

His hand on my other shoulder, he lifts me to my feet. "I'm wondering if you're ready to walk out of here. You feel like you can deal with this later?" He gestures at the horse with his chin.

I have to think. There's the horse, and here I am. I wonder if I can do it later. It's my job, I figure. I'll go to the tent truck and get some spare line. I'll round up a crew and take care of this.

And tomorrow we'll break down the tent. Tomorrow we'll drive off for a new season. Another season.

There's a pain in my gut worse than before. Something I can't identify. Halfway out into the blinding day, it hits me.

I'm jealous of the horse.

July
1987

▲

Independence Day

▲

Tonight, across the county road, in the center of the dog-racing track, all of Bitter Springs will gather for fireworks and speeches.

Bitter Springs is the third-largest beef-processing city in the Northeast. We've been parked behind the slaughterhouse for thirteen days.

Generally we'd be moving on after three days, but after Circus Argo's bleachers collapsed up north, towns started to panic. First, Reform canceled, then Paradise. Fabrizio cut a deal. We could stay in Bitter Springs through Independence Day. We'd set up in the slaughterhouse parking lot, and ten percent of each ticket sold would go toward new jerseys for the high school football team.

This is Bitter Springs's 250th anniversary, and we are part of the Gala Independence Birthday celebration. Sponsored by the Beef King Prime Cuts factory, the slaughterhouse that employs most of the town. You get a great view of the loading docks from the backlot.

▲

The small parking lot chokes our trailers between razor-wire fences. It's crowded with sleepers and animals and laundry lines. We tiptoe round elephant and horse dung, mud puddles from leaky water hoses. Hay bales send dust and mites into the greasy air. Townie children lean over the yellow security fence and throw bones at us. They laugh and run away.

Trucks pull up to the loading dock, inches from the fence that separates our shower truck from the real world. A parade of cows, nose to butt, stroll on rubber nonskid pads through the plastic-strip doors. Slaughterhouse employees, boys too young to work inside on the line, herd them through the door with sapling switches. But the cows ignore them, stay in line on their own. March inside on their own. The motions of these boys in rust jumpers are all for show.

All day long animals parade through the Beef King factory doors. Cows, pigs, horses. They walk in, up ramps, on the hoof. They leave on steel rollers, meat slabs packaged in plastic rolling out through a curtain of frosty plastic strips. Boys toss them onto refrigerated trucks backed up to the loading dock. Meat in, meat out. Meat in, meat out. Whistle blows, shift change. A steady stream of processing. Never ends.

Meat in, meat out.

After our first week, the electrician and the soundman were fined for urinating in the street. They were drinking at Joe's, and the townies wouldn't let them use the bathroom. The next day some local kids spray-painted the gennie: "Circus go home." Tattoo Lou's groom was caught snatching panties from backyard laundry lines. The police said they wouldn't hold him after Tom shook hands with a fifty folded in his palm. There have been scuffles over Joe's pool table, and more than a few shoving matches. Tahar says someone threw rocks at his elephants. Ivory has a nick over her eye. We're sick of this town, and it's sick of us.

The slaughterhouse sits on one side of the circus; on the other sits Joe's Meat Market. After a shift ends, townies pour from the locker room doors and head across the parking lot to Joe's. They skirt around our yellow security fence, bitching that we're in the way, when will we move on? They moan when we enter Joe's, say it's a locals' bar and who gave us the right to use up their air? But that doesn't stop me from going over this morning. I tell myself I'm going to celebrate Independence Day.

Joe's Meat Market is a cold, dark cave despite the bright heat outside. My eyes swim through red haze a moment, taking time to adjust. The bar is fairly crowded. Off-shift townies. The young ones without families to pack picnics for. Some older men chugging a few beers before family barbecues.

Jay leans against the spongy wood bar, his thigh woven tight with Tattoo Lou's. She whispers something in Jay's ear, cleans it out with her tongue, and he tilts his head towards hers. Christmas lights blink on and off in the window. The glass panes have been painted black; the lights, once jewel-colored, are now faded to pastel. They blink on every three seconds, hold for one second, then flick off. One-two, off three. One-two, off three.

The dining area, where women sit in clusters or cower before enormous men, is simply a jumble of dark gray slate tables on single steel poles planted into rocking steel disks. The girls in Joe's Meat Market are tiny; I could crush them in one fist. Their legs are smooth under tight miniskirts. Their lipstick is candy-colored and glossy, like magazine pages. I bet they have poodle names: Bebe, Sandee, Cherri.

I feel conspicuous in my faded pocket tee and Carhartt overalls. The smell of diesel rises from the oily stains on the mustard fabric, and I feel like a sign is painted on my forehead: MONKEY GIRL. In the old gold curlicue style of carnival freak show posters.

This morning I overheard Jay, Tattoo Lou, and Bo talking about me. First laughter, then Jay's voice, clear and loud: "Fucking her is like fucking a little boy."

I was under the side grandstand, mending a garbage net with seine twine. I froze, twine mid-knot. My breath rattled. I hoped they couldn't hear. Jay and Bo were raking the ringdirt into graceful swirls; they didn't see me hidden only twenty feet away, listening.

"No, wait—it's like fucking a statue of a little boy!" I crouched in the shadows, peeking through the spaces between the bleacher boards. Bo bent to his rake; his face didn't twitch to show his opinion, one way or the other.

Tattoo Lou straddled the ringcurb, sipping coffee from a Styrofoam cup. She said, "Hairy little monkey. She was!" Her voice raised so Bo, pretending not to listen, could hear.

"You can have her if you want her. We make no claim." Jay raked himself up onto the curb. He kissed Lou on her white scalp. I slipped under the sidewall and came here.

"Hey, Mat. Matty, wake up." Tom calls to me. A fast-burning Marlboro is wedged between the stumps of his left hand. The cigarette flares and hisses every few moments, like it's smoking itself. His blond hair, darkened by dirt and grease, falls over dull eyes. He's been here awhile. He points to an empty chair. Blue paint chips from the overly upright back. I sit across from him, rest my forearms lightly on the slate. The whole table rocks a bit, till it's caught by the folded matchbook wedged under the leg. On his right, a dirty little girl, maybe six or seven, still padded in baby fat, perches on her muddy heels. Her hands work around two hard plastic dolls; her lips move with some whispered story. The man doll has black hair and wears only a suit jacket. Nothing covers his smooth naked pelvis. The female doll has long straight blond hair, wears pants that match the jacket; her breasts, unnatural nippleless cones, jut out between the child's knuckles.

"Pavement came up to say hello last night." Tom chuckles a bit, touches his swollen lips gingerly.

The man behind the bar—he cooks, cleans, mixes drinks, and rents videos, so he must be Joe, though he never speaks enough to tell us his name, and when we try to buy him drinks he always says, "Not tonight"—he looks up and then goes back to wiping foam off the soggy bar.

"You know Bo, Mat?" The ember of Tom's Marlboro draws a red arrow in the smoke, points towards a man in jungle fatigues. His name tag and insignia have been ripped off, and none too carefully. Threads still dangle in rectangular and oval outlines. Bo's hair is the same color as the slate table slabs. There's no name for that color of hair. It curls in long strands around his thick shoulders. He holds them shut close, tight, like he's hiding his flabby pectorals. They droop like unformed adolescent breasts. It's not that he's fat, it's just he's woefully out of shape, or perhaps he was fat once and this loose flesh is what's left over, after a quick drop in weight. His eyes, too, are the colorless dark of a lead pencil. A helmet of scabs covers his chin. He is not the kind of man who can have his pick of women. He's the kind that should be grateful if any show him the time of day. The kind that would be faithful.

"You had us strapping down trucks together last move, remember?" I say.

Tom pinches his swollen nose tenderly with his good

hand. "I can't remember shit anymore. We've been in this goddamn town so long I've forgotten everything that came before."

"Well, we did," I say. We never spoke. Wordlessly, Bo threw unrolling straps over the load to me. On the other side, I threaded the hard melted edge through the ratchet and cranked the webbing down tight. After we finished all the flatbeds, he'd said, "You got the prettiest blue eyes, Mat. Why don't you and me make a baby?"

"Okay," I said.

He pushed me up against the tent truck, my head squeezed between his soft hands. Sharp steel truckbed pressed into my shoulder blades. I opened my arms to him, to take him in a soft way, but he pushed his mouth hard up on mine. His teeth grinding against mine, no room for lips or tongues. He hurt me. I wanted him to kiss differently, more like Jay. I slipped my hand into his jeans. I thought if I made him feel different, he'd kiss different. But I didn't do it right; he stayed small and soft.

He pushed himself off me and said, "You know, Mat, I'm more interested in how you feel inside than how it feels inside you."

I didn't know what to say. I didn't know what he meant. Later, I was sorry. Maybe I could've shown him how to kiss, or he could've told me what he wanted. That was nearly two weeks ago, and we haven't spoken since.

"It's no good to stay in one place so long," Tom says, mostly to himself. His voice snaps me out of a stare. In my mind I was following Lou's hand into the waistband of Jay's jeans. I help myself to one of Tom's Marlboros.

He picks bits of dried blood from his elbow, checks the progress of his nose scab with his fingertips. "Boredom will be the end of us, mark my word."

"I'd come home, but I'm afraid that you won't take me back; but I'd give up everything just to have you near." A man at the bar sings along with the jukebox.

I slide my eyes from the Tibetan wheel on Lou's exposed shoulder to the 250 beer labels on the wood paneled wall.

"Read the labels to Mat, Bo," Tom commands. "Bo reads real well," he says behind a cupped hand, as if this were an embarrassing secret.

Bo reads the labels out loud for me, one at a time, in a slow meditative voice. "Corona, Tecate, Harp, Guinness . . . "

He's slightly younger than Jay, but his meaty face has the set frozen stiffness of someone very old. No one would mistake him for handsome. But when he reads, he could be mistaken for kind. Concentration softens his face. And I'm a sucker for a man who reads to me. Soon I'm lost on the rising falling tide of his voice reciting beer names.

". . . Coors, Miller, Saranac, Sapporo . . . " His voice betrays Appalachian roots. Like hot honey, his drawl drips into my ear. ". . . Dos Equis, Bass, Red Wolf, Wicked Ale . . . "

Joe the barman finally lumbers over, his heavy thighs buckling knobby knees inward, his calves, ankles, and feet splayed out for balance. I order Uncle Jack's Hard Cider. Not a real beer, more like sweet apple fizz.

Bo says, "A lady drink for a lady." We lift our bottles in cheers.

"Who's this?" I ask Tom, tilting my bottle towards the child.

"This is Tammy," his battered face smiley, his voice a happy singsong. Tammy ignores him. His tone drops, a whisper he thinks she can't hear, but I notice the dolls freeze in her hand while he explains.

"My sister-in-law's kid. Her husband's been getting all

kinds of drunk and it's been getting real messy, so Bea, that's Patsy's sister, dropped Tammy off with us for a bit. Bea's planning on hooking up with a Ren-fest. She got a beer and mead concession. Once she makes a little money, they can move in with her mom. And we got the kid till then."

"An' this is Ken an' this is Barbie." Tammy holds up each doll in turn.

"Pleased to meet you," I say. But they're already hitting each other with stiff plastic straight-arm fists.

"How old is she?" I ask.

"Six."

The empties hit the table. We order again, with a flick of Tom's fingerless hand.

At the small table nearest me, a skinny woman with marshmallow hair grips the large paw of her beef-fed date in her small hand. He drops her fingers to drink his beer. With a cocktail stirrer, she tears her cuticles, yellowed from years on the slaughter line. I look to see if she draws blood with her pointy straw. She lays down her stirrer and paints the nails deep brick, a color to camouflage stains from dried entrails. The sharp smell of nail polish drifts over to our table, and Tammy wrinkles her nose.

Another round. We move into shots. Kamikazes.

The tiny woman with marshmallow hair begins in a nasal voice, "So the manager calls me into his office and says this college kid wants a whole beef heart. . . . So I says, 'What the hell does he want that for?' And he says, 'How the hell would I know? You talk to him. . . .'"

The worn dartboard has so many holes it won't hold a dart, and the plastic fire is useless on this warm July day, but I'm almost content and getting a tingly warm buzz.

"... turns out he needs it for a art project for school, see? He's a art major, see? So I says, 'Look, kid, my job is inspect the hearts, and I gotta do that by cutting them open, see? Right down the middle.'"

We take turns buying, feeling generous, simply a gesture. Meaningless. We may as well run our own tabs. We know it will all even out in the end.

Barbie and Ken fight, kiss and make up, and split up again. My stomach glows with liquor-filled goodwill. I swear I can see past Bo's worn-down flesh to the handsome bones underneath.

"Worms, I gotta stop the whole thing. USDA, you know?" The heart-cutter's voice fills my ears. "But this kid, does he get it? No. I'm in the manager's office, and this kid wants me slipping a uncut heart in my pocket."

Tammy has five sweaty ice-filled highball glasses in front of her. She collects the maraschino cherries and orange slices from her Shirley Temples on a cocktail napkin.

The heart-cutter's story fades away, and I ride waves of music and booze.

Tom doubles up; drinking two to every one of mine.

Bo says, "They did this study. Most violent workplaces are slaughterhouses. Post offices come in distant second. Something 'bout whacking all those carcasses over and over. Hardens a person somehow. Blood loses meaning. Wears out the part of their brain that understands pain or something."

On the paneled walls, a stuffed goose wears a necktie, a coyote in sunglasses and a baseball cap kisses a stuffed buck's neck.

"'S name's Bo-regard," Tom says suddenly. "Means

handsome-look. You two could make some pretty babies."
He downs his shot and waves at Joe. Joe ignores him.

"Wan' another apple-soda beer, Mat? Get Mat another,
Bo," Tom says. "She's the best, Mat's the best. Like a daughter she is. The best. Get her anything she wants, on me." He
slaps a fiver on the table and says, "I'ma go back to the li'l
lady. You take care of this 'ere li'l lady."

I watch him sway towards the door. On his way past the
bar he slams his lobster-claw hand on the bar. Five wet slaps.

"Hey-hey-hey-hey-hey!" He bangs right under Joe's nose.
"Serve the lady. My money's no good here? My money's
good, goddammit! Just as good as any 'merican's . . . "

"Get outta here, ya stinkin' drunk," the townie with the
marshmallow-haired date yells.

"Stinkin' townies. Com'ere an' say'at. . . ," Tom mumbles,
and swings the heavy door open. He pauses for a moment,
stalled by the sudden bright sun outside. The people in the
bar, townies and roustabouts alike, all look up from their
drinks, eyes frozen by the brightness, like deer caught in the
glare of a semi's headlights. As if we'd all forgot it was still
early afternoon. Tom becomes a black cutout hole plastered
against white afternoon. Then the door shuts behind him,
and we blink in the dim light again. Joe spits on the floor
and wipes at the spot where Tom slapped the bar.

Bo lifts Tom's half-smoked cigarette from the pie-plate
aluminum ashtray and draws a long inhale. The tip flares
up hot and red. Tammy lifts her cocktail straw to her pouty
lips, eyes on Bo, a deep inhale.

He switches his grip to pinch the butt between thumb
and forefinger, then brings it down on the soft white flesh of
his inner forearm. The faintest sizzle of downy hairs burning, a charred bacon-wool smell; a slight grimace crosses his

face. Tammy freezes, straw perched over her arm, mouth parted in a wide unspoken oh. I let my breath out slowly, waiting for his next move. He is a different kind of man from Jay; I don't want to make any more mistakes with him.

He says, "It hurts worst the first time, but after a while it gets easier."

He smokes the cigarette to the filter; he watches clear fluid filling the angry red-gray crater in his skin.

"Tante says burnt roses smell just like burning flesh. She should know." I'm speaking to fill the air between us. "Her husband burned over three-quarters of her body." Bo looks up. I continue. "He threw cooking oil on her. She's lucky to have hair." His eyes drop back to his arm. My fingers itch to touch his burn hole.

"This is nothing." He gestures to the pit. It's the newest in a row of scabs and scars.

"Mmm." I nod my head, half yes, half no.

"You know I was a POW in Nam? The shit they did there . . . after a while physical pain means nothing. It got so I could get lost in a fly on the wall, a crack in the floor. Just pull myself into it and not feel a thing. Now, sometimes, I do this"—he holds up the smoking filter—"just to remember I'm still alive."

I shrug, still casual. But inside I think: Sounds right.

He's telling a story now. His voice has that rhythm that denies reply. Barbie and Ken lie still, listening.

"You know, I never thought I was gonna live this long. I wasn't supposed to. When I got out of Nam, still alive, I thought: Well, God, that's it now; I'm done, right? I kept waiting for a truck to hit me, or the doctor to tell me I got bone cancer or some gook-killer parasite, but I just kept on going. If my life was a good movie, the credits would've started rolling when I walked out that prison camp. I'd be walking into the sunset, movie over. But here I am, with all these years. Like God's pulling a big joke on me." He downs his drink. "I'm so bored."

Jay puts a quarter in the jukebox and pulls Lou into a small space between the bar and the front tables. Jay's arm drapes loosely over the school of salmon swimming upstream along Lou's spine.

> *"Wasted and wounded*
> *ain't what the moon did,*
> *got what I paid for now . . . "*

Tom Waits laments, and Jay's and Lou's hips swing together.

I feel Bo watching me; out of the corner of my eye I see him turn around in his chair to see who I'm staring at.

Without moving my eyes to catch his, I say, "It's not true. Whatever Jay and Lou say about me, it's not true." I press my knee against Bo's under the table.

"I don't give a shit what anyone says about anyone," Bo says. "Come on, you wanna dance? I know you wanna dance." He stands up, blocking my view of Jay and Lou, and I realize my knee is only pressing against the table stand.

"Don't move," I warn Tammy. My finger points stiffly at her nose, like the motherly fingers of townie women warning their children not to wander near the elephants or eat too much candy.

His arms around my neck, mine around his lower back, we shift our weight from foot to foot. I bury my chin in his fatigues and stare over his shoulder. He smells like smoke and mildew.

"I'm an innocent victim
of a blinded alley
and I'm tired of all these soldiers here . . . "

The music's a funeral dirge. Bo kneads my shoulders with ham hock hands, whispers in my ear, "You're really wound tight. Relax. I'll give you a massage."

I shrug my shoulders against his heavy hands.

"Massages make me tense," I say.

He strokes the rigid muscle and bone. "You know what tension is? It's built-up anger."

From our table, Barbie scolds, "Ken, where you been?"

Ken pleads, "Aw babybaby puh-leeze . . . I promise . . . "

Lou leans her head against Jay's neck, I lean mine against Bo's. It's a relief to finally lean against a man again.

"You're really mad at Jay, aren't you, Mat." Lou brushes Jay's cheek with her lips, I brush my lips against Bo's jaw.

Barbie and Ken wrestle on the table. Tammy does both voices, shrill and loud. Ken: "You lyin' cheatin' nogood." Barbie: "Ima hurtyoubad."

Bo whispers into my scalp, "If you could, you'd hurt him real bad, wouldn't you?" His pelvis presses against my ribcage; he's that much taller than me. I pretend I don't feel the heat building there, the hard movement. I wonder what Tammy sees. If Tammy can hear what he's saying over the music. I wonder why he can get it up now, in this public place, talking shit, and he couldn't when we were alone, pressed together against the flatbed, when I was ready and willing to take him in. I wonder if maybe he's got something wrong with him. But it's just so nice to be touched again. It's so hard to go so long without touch.

". . . I begged you to stab me,
you tore my shirt open,
and I'm down on my knees tonight . . . "

I concentrate on the gravel lyrics, the scratchy record-ing, the hard slate under the balls of my feet, the red glow behind the lids of my eyes.

"You ever think of killing someone, Mat? I bet you get really angry. I bet you're really angry at Jay. You want to hurt him? I heard what they did to you. . . ." His movements are more insistent.

I look past his shoulder, like looking into a broken mir-ror, a thousand confusions. All the noises, the lights. His penis pushes against my stomach, harder.

Ken holds Barbie's face to the candle. She melts in soft screams. A scarred and wrinkled old woman. Tammy hisses a pretend scream through clenched teeth.

"You want to hurt Jay? I bet you're really angry at him. You want to hurt him? You want to get angry?" It's the talk; the talk turns him on. Maybe I could just let him talk and ignore it. He grinds into me. Hard cider soured by stomach bile rises in my throat. "You could get angry at me. You could hurt me, I wouldn't feel it," he says.

I push my hands against his insistent hips, push him off me, duck my head through his circling arms. Two steps to the table. I search my sleeve for my rolled-up pack of Luckies.

"Are you trying to freak me out?" I say. "Because if you are, you'll have to try a little harder." My movements are jerky; I put out two matches before I manage to light my cig-arette. "It might work on some other girls, but I'm not that easy to scare. I'm a little tougher than that. Is this how you get turned on?"

The thrashings of the dolls slow. Tammy watches, more interested in our fight.

Bo drops his voice. "I was just checking to see where you're at, Mat. You're just a kid." He sits. I lower myself carefully into my chair, eyes on him the whole time. "You don't even know what you want." His tone is as empty as if he's reading a list of beers.

"I do too know what I want," I answer, surprised at my childish tone.

"Oh yeah? What's that?"

I look down at the Lucky burning in my hand, duck my head to hide the heat creeping across my cheeks.

"You don't have the guts to tell me." Bo lifts my head, with his fingers under my chin. His touch is gentle now. I'm surprised by the warm drop in my guts, the vague sexual quiver in my crotch. His touch feels different from before. He orders another round.

The drinks arrive, but no one drinks. Tammy fishes the fruit out of hers and wraps it in the napkin, soggy with her other saved cherries and oranges. I hold Bo's unsteady gaze. Things could go either way. We could fuck, or fight. I'm not sure which I want, and I'm not sure he cares.

"Come on, Tammy." I grab her elbow and jerk her from the seat. "We got to ask Tom if I can take you to the fire-works."

"I'm sorry," Bo says. "I think I've had too much." He folds his arms and lays his head on the table. His hair spills across the slate. Maybe it was just the drink talking before. He looks helpless, open to any townie violence. I'm not sure what to do. His back shudders. I wonder if he's crying. I touch him between the shoulder blades softly. He doesn't respond.

"Bo?" I ask. His name feels so strange in my mouth, I think it may be the first time I've said it.

"Sorry," he says. "Later."

I move the drinks away from his elbows so he won't knock them over and get himself wet. His breathing evens out, slows. I figure he's sleeping.

Finally I take Tammy's hand and lead her through the tables, careful not to bump any townies.

As I pass the bar, a townie man says, "You know why these little bastards burn so damn fast?" I turn quickly, sure he's saying something about me. But he's holding his cigarette to Joe's eye level. "It's the saltpeter those cheaters mix in the tobacco."

"Isn't that what they put in college kids' food so they won't wanna have sex?" Joe asks.

I open the heavy wood and iron door onto a bright afternoon. The light blinds me.

The slaughterhouse has closed early for the celebration. For once the smell of dying cows and pigs is overwhelmed by the smell of barbecued chicken and buttered corn. I'm taking Tammy to the fireworks. A light wind carries the squeals of suburban children running under cold sprinklers, music playing from tinny backyard radios.

We run across the two-lane county road.

"Why can't we bring Tom?" Tammy whines, dragging her feet.

I yank the little girl by a sweaty palm along the sidewalk. "Your uncle feels sick."

She fits her toes gingerly between cracks.

Small paper packets of firecrackers pop-pop-pop, startling Tammy each time. But she loves collecting the singed blue and green paper shreds that litter the sidewalk. Soon her pockets overflow with these burnt treasures.

The sidewalk opens on a grassy field three-quarters

around the oval dog track. On one long side are fifteen tiers of bleachers. Some families have set up in the bleachers, some inside the track itself.

At the short north end of the track, the football team stands on a flatbed truck decorated with red, white, and blue crepe paper. I lean against a tree at the south curve, away from the townie crowd. The gray track separates us. Tammy plays with Barbie and Ken in the fine dry dust at my feet.

Post-picnic, families lounge and chat, waiting for dark. Styrofoam coolers, plates, and plastic flatware litter the grass. Children wave cheap cotton flags on wooden sticks. Sparklers and punks flash fiery patterns in the fading evening.

A man in a burgundy fez makes a speech, the microphone booms and whines: ". . . fine youth . . . future of our fair country . . . family values . . . America . . . "

Now comes the Valedictorian, the Quarterback, the Homecoming Queen. Cheerleaders lead a cheer, maroon panties and white pom-poms flashing. The crowd joins in, loud and garbled.

Two vets, Bitter Springs's oldest and youngest, are led up onto the stage. The old, white-haired man stands straight-backed behind the younger man, who is poured softly in a wheelchair. They receive medals on ribbons. The mayor stoops to place the medal around the young man's neck.

". . . served their country well . . . " I notice Bo, swaying slightly. Standing at attention, saluting the soldiers. The band plays "America the Beautiful."

Darkness, black night before the moon rises. Then explosions. Millions of tiny burning sparks. All the colors light the sky, then fall safely cold to the ground. I crouch with my back against a tree. Tammy leans against my knees. Slowly, through small shifts I barely notice, her little warm body folds itself into my lap.

A red fireball, then squiggly silver sparks that whistle when they fall. Tammy points to them and calls them "fishies."

"Why fishies?" I ask.

"I don't know; that's just what my ma calls them," she says.

Overhead a blue waterfall is broken by three green bursts.

Tammy sits up and twists around to face me. "What if my ma doesn't come for me?" she asks.

I stroke her hair behind her ears and sigh. "I suppose you'd live with Tom and Patsy. And then you and me could be best friends."

"No we couldn't. You're too old."

"Well then, I'd be like your big sister."

She still shakes her head no.

"I could be your aunt?"

"Okay." She scrunches her butt down into my lap and settles back.

We watch the fireworks. I like the gold showers best; they remind me of the Disney films my ma used to take me to.

Tammy falls asleep. The fireworks end in a messy and loud finale. She stirs but doesn't open her eyes, and I find I've been rocking, looking at her closed eyelids. I didn't even see the picnickers leave. The dog track is empty now, except for blowing litter. I carry Tammy back to the lot, my arms a cradle, Barbie and Ken stuffed into my back pockets.

Tom and Patsy's trailer is dark and empty, but Tammy is sound asleep. I tuck her into the dinette bed and perch her dolls on the windowsill so she can find them first thing in the morning.

Arms now empty, my body feels lonely and cold. I don't want to sleep alone.

Naked, I climb into Bo's bed. I lie under the sheets, waiting for him to return. Time passes in a half drowse. Then a new weight on the mattress wakes me.

He lies down on top of the blankets, stiff and fully clothed. He smells of greasepaint and mildewed cloth. Of damp soil and pavement tar, like he's been crawling on his stomach. His sweat is sharp and pungent, the sweat of nerves, not hard work. That and the undertone of meat that hovers around this whole town follow him in the trailer.

Into the dark sleeper he says, "My sergeant used to tell me, 'One day you're gonna come around the corner and meet yourself,' and I didn't know what he meant until I met you, Mat."

I cup my breasts in callused hands, feel my heart beating fast. I clench my legs together under his sheets. I think: Maybe we are meant for each other. Maybe here's the person who won't leave. Maybe, after we've been together awhile, the sight of Jay and Lou won't stab me. Maybe we'll have a little girl who can play with Tammy.

He lies rigid. Only his lips and tongue move, barely forming the question: "Why are you here?"

I curl my toes and tense my jaw. Now the question's been asked, I wonder this myself. Jay never asked. He always just knew what to do.

"This afternoon, in the bar, you said things . . . In the tent, this morning . . . I saw you at the fireworks . . . " I stammer.

"What do you want?" he asks.

I take a deep breath and steady my thoughts.

"If we had a baby, I'd keep it. You wouldn't have to do anything. I take good care of Tammy. I could—"

He lifts his hand suddenly. Stop, it says.

I flinch. Then wait, wondering if I've made a mistake. A stiffness creeps into my shoulders, and my brain repeats the words, You asshole, you've done it again. You fucked up again.

But his hand floats gently down on his chest, and he sighs like an old man.

"You're like an open wound. You walk up to men with your shirt open, saying, Here's my heart, step on it."

I have no idea what he's talking about. Jay never spoke like this. Bo's crazy. I lie quietly, waiting for some behavior I recognize, so I'll know how to react.

"You better get out of here. I don't have what you need." He swings his feet off the bed and stands with his back to me, nose inches from the sleeper door. "I'll wait outside while you get dressed. Just take your pain and go home."

He steps outside, leaving the door slightly open. A thin slice of the full moon paints a white streak across the floor. The light creeps slowly towards the bunk. I begin to understand, vaguely, faintly. I'm being sent away.

He's sending me away.

Now my muscles take on the dead heavy weight of a carcass hung to age on steel hooks. I can barely lift my useless limbs from his cold bed. Dressing, I shake from the effort of movement.

The wet silver night is empty. He must be hiding from me, so I must have reason to be ashamed. I arrive at the idea of shame through this reasoning.

Beads of moisture hang in the air, too light to fall to the ground. From far away, I watch my body walk through the clouds.

There's a light on in the costume truck. Tante's up late. She bends over a white enamel basin, the bright round moon her only light. Over and over, she dips tights into water. The water turns a darker pink with each rinse. Now, in the dark damp costume truck, I'm frightened like I was as a child. The old woman's scars have only grown deeper over the years, accentuated by wrinkles and scowls. Her face has melted and caved in on itself, the long nose collapsing towards her chin, cheekbones cutting through tissue-thin skin. Eyebrows never grew back where they burned off so long ago. Her sharp dark eye is lashless; the other, an empty socket hidden behind a black patch.

"I saw him again tonight, that crazy man," she says. She doesn't have to turn her head to know I'm there, who it is. Her long nose knows my smell.

"He crawls on his belly with a gun. Tom should take it away, run the crazy off." She hangs the tights on a wooden rack and reaches for another pair.

"Why are you up so late, Tante?" I ask.

"Wash by the moon. You know nothing." She clucks and mumbles to the basin. "The moon draws its own, the moon blood. To get rid of stains, wash by the moon. You know nothing of being a woman, Mat."

"That's crazy," I say, turning away.

"I'm crazy." She laughs hard, first a sandpaper rasp, finally ending in a full crow cackle. "I'm crazy, she says! She who just crawled out from a crazy man's bed."

I try to think of an excuse, but she cuts me off.

"Don't bother; I saw you leave his sleeper." Her voice

now softens to a grandmother's tone. "It took me so long to learn, Mat. I was like you. Do the same thing over and over, thinking it will be different. You think one man's gonna save you from another man? Now who is crazy?"

She makes no sense to me. I wonder if we have all gone insane. Finally the old woman looks up through the veil of her fallen white mane, loosed from the angry knot at the nape of her deeply scarred neck. An illusion, for a moment she looks younger, whispering like a young woman to her lover. Her lipless mouth breathes soft words through her webbed fingers.

"At night I see him patrolling. Like the soldiers when I was a girl. Like the soldiers back home. In the camouflage clothes. His face in paint. He patrols the grounds." Her ash-gray eye sparks. "He's a crazy one, that one."

"Good night, Tante," I say, careful to keep my voice respectful.

"Wait. You want to know crazy? I'll tell you crazy. Bo was never in the war. You know how come Tom calls him Scambo?" She steps to the door, throws the basin of bloody water into the yard. Moonlight glints off her shiny scar tissue.

"No," I answer.

"He was born in '59. That means he was 18 in '77. He missed it. Too late. Your man is a liar."

I don't understand the numbers she's throwing at me. "Who told you?"

"Tom. He has all the papers, the ID. The story Bo tells, it's from nothing. The man, he is crazy. Has memories of a war he wasn't in." She laughs again. My heart skips, then speeds up to make up for lost beats.

"But he knows so much," I say. I dig my nails into the flesh inside my elbow.

"Yes, crazy people will surprise you. What they know.

Touched by God." She makes a cross over her flat breasts and touches her forehead. She fills the basin with clean water from a pitcher and reaches for another pair of tights.

"He just kicked me out his bed," I confess. These words are dry on my tongue.

"Why do you keep going to men, Matilda?" She spits as if something bitter dropped in her mouth.

I sneer, sarcastic, picturing Tattoo Lou's dancing back in Jay's arms. "Are women any different?"

"He is scum. He has insulted you."

I barely hear her; my ears are ringing, roaring, clogged with pounding blood. Something in my lungs struggles to break through my ribs. I step backwards, away from Tante's sharp eye. Heavy costumes close around me. I push at velvet and gauze, scratchy sequined tulle. Ringdirt, loosed from the fabric, chokes me.

"They're all scum," I say, teeth grinding. Fists clenching. Pa, Jay, Lou, Bo. All scum.

"He's not worth the dust on your heels, Matilda. My child." Red bleeds into the basin. "He should pay for his disrespect. I could show him, but I am too old." A dry laugh like stale leaking air from a punctured tire. "Make them all pay."

I back down the truck's ramp.

The generator is off; all the trailers and sleepers are dark. But the bigtop glows softly under the full moon. Props squat around its back door, dark shadowy things. Electric cables snake out from under the sidewall, tendrils waiting to trip me.

I walk away slowly, holding my body stiff.

At my back, Tante's calling, "Hoo, you are angry now! That's a good girl. That's my girl. Now use it! This is your strength!"

Take your pain and go home ... take your pain and go home ... This is the rhythm I walk in. It grows large and fills my brain. Now I run. My heels pound the parking lot pavement, but I feel nothing. I tear around the stakeline. Take your pain and go home. Past the concessions tents. Take your pain and go home. In the midway, looking past the entrance tent to Joe's, I slam back into my skin.

Hot electric blood pounds in my temples. Pulse speeds like I just took a hit of crystal. My eyes have night vision, my muscles new power. Air jumps into my lungs, begging to be breathed; it tastes clean and cold. The ground rises up to catch my steady feet. I move with the grace and strength of a prized stallion through the gate, out the circus lot. Running down the short length of cracked sidewalk, the circus behind me. Running to Joe's. Every night noise, every shadow, is new and thrilling. I am furious.

The heavy wood door of Joe's Meat Market slams against the wall. Heads of townies turn, their faces open with surprise. The bar is lined with men drinking alone and in groups, here for post-firework beers. Their women are probably home tucking overtired children in bed.

I step in enough for the door to swing shut behind me, but not far enough to order a drink. I have an announcement.

I could break the bar by slamming my fists down, I could flip tables over one-handed. I could smash a man's nose to the back of his head and laugh with the pleasure and exhilaration of it.

Instead, shifting my weight from foot to foot like a boxer, I shout, "Listen up, I'm only gonna say this once." As I've heard Tom and Jay yell at their crews so many times.

They put their beers down and wait.

"Who's got a wife or a girlfriend named Bebe or Staci or Sally or something like that? About so high"—I wave my hand from my shoulder to my chin—"with reddish or blondish or light-brown hair. Pretty. Tight jeans, makeup, gold jewelry, youngish?" I have described nearly every woman under thirty in this town, and I know it. Recognition creeps over a few dull faces.

"You mean Kiki?" someone calls from the back.

"Maybe," I answer. "Or maybe Mimi."

"Fuckin' Mimi . . . what?"

"She's getting screwed by a roustabout named Bo in sleeper twelve. I won't tell you again, and I wasn't here," I say, turning to leave. "Sleeper twelve. Bo," I tell them again.

Then I run out the door. The sounds of cursing and heavy glass pints slamming the sodden bar thrill up and down my spine.

I run to my sleeper and fall onto my bunk. I am laughing, happy and free. Rolling in the mattress, hugging my pillow.

I wish Al was here to celebrate with me. My best friend, my sister. He should be here for my victory. He's probably hiding in the cookhouse, hoarding a bottle all to himself. I'll tell him in the morning. How I made Bo pay. He'll say, "You go, girl!" and give me three snaps. I bounce on the mattress like a child. I can't wait to tell him.

"Look who's on top now!" I say out loud to the empty sleeper. I laugh myself clean. The warmth of safety and calm, joy and content, covers my tired bones. I breathe evenly. I could fall easily asleep.

Instead I pinch my arms to stay alert. I sit on the lower bunk, waiting for something to begin. A sledgehammer handle by my side, my knife in my pocket; I am ready.

I rock with adrenaline. "A hundred bottles of beer on

the wall, a hundred bottles of beer . . . " I sing the song I've heard audience children sing, to pass the time.

At seventy-seven, I'm interrupted by pounding on the sleeper door and cries of "Hey Rube!"

"Hey Rube!" echoes through the lot, down sleeper row. Our war cry. It means there's a fight with outsiders, it means circus folk in need of help, it means battle-ready, everyone on his feet.

I jump from my bunk, the sledgehammer handle already clenched in my fist. I feel alive.

I pull back the door-window curtain and peer into dark. The moon has hidden behind clouds. The faint outline of the sleeper directly across from me, parked not five feet away, barely shows itself. A row of numbered doors with windows, a row of metal stairs. My view of the rest of the lot is blocked by this closely parked sleeper. I can't see the damage yet.

But the noise! Sounds fall into my ears. Crashing and screaming, and fists banging aluminum siding. Things breaking, the flat slaps of rubber running on asphalt, the hollow clomps of wood clogs tripping. Flesh slams against steel stairs. Elephants trumpet, horses whinny, people scream. The rising pitch of the attacker. The falling pitch of the hit. I wait for a break in the nearby noise and take in my last deep breath.

I enter the night slowly, careful to lock the door behind, so I won't return home only to be jumped by someone hiding in my bed.

Quietly, I move through the maze of the crowded back-lot. Step over stairs, water hoses, electricity cables. Sliding along the sleeper, always protecting my back so I only have to defend my front. Swinging my head 180 degrees, side to side, handle raised ready. But sleeper row is empty.

At the end of sleeper row, I step into the midway.

The open space between concessions stands is the chosen battleground. Between the balloon tree and the candy floss wagon, shadows smash together, fall apart.

A concessions wagon tips on its side. It crashes to the cement. The popcorn popper shatters. Hotdogs and buns bounce across the midway. Townies run out from behind the tipped wagon. Ketchup and mustard packets squirt beneath their feet. They slip in the goo, laughing, whooping. Electricians and concessionaires chase them, tackle them. They roll through mounds of popped corn.

More unfamiliar bodies, townies, rage past a closed-up toy tent, hollering, "Motherfucker, you're gonna die. Fucker!" Afghani tumblers meet them halfway, stakes raised overhead. The ringcrew joins in, swinging rakes and pitchforks.

Behind the box-office trailer, the Mexican catcher beats a townie with a wrench. Bleacher boys rush past, metal in hand. Chains, tire irons, seatback risers meet arms, chests, heads. The toy tent is pushed over, and a flood of plastic souvenirs, magic wands, and costumed dolls spill onto the pavement.

This is more than I pictured.

I run around the bigtop, invisible in its shadow. A siren of senseless noise streams from my open mouth. I'm filled with a new power. Any sense of safety, any sense of sense, has flown from my newly awakened body. I smash the handle down on scalps, shoulders, noses. Cracks and thuds. Some deep old part of me craves the sound of wood splitting flesh. Teeth, blood, hair. I bellow, I scream.

"You fuckers! You're all gonna pay!" The words rise from my belly of their own accord. I trot round to the backlot. Trip a townie, step on his neck. His eyes are wide and scared. I bring the handle down on his cheekbone.

There are so many ways to hurt. Ideas fill my head, and I sculpt them, in real skin and tissue, with whoever crosses me. As each goes down, I get higher. This must be how it feels to be a man. To slap your woman. To rip a hymen. To thrust and break me open. Watch me cry, bleed. I get it now. It's my turn.

Quiet, I slow my breath, stalk with the soft killer paws of the lion.

"Oh-god-help, oh-god-help." Behind the shower truck, I trip over a prone body chanting, clutching his guts. Moon shines on blood. I don't recognize his face. Not-circus. Townie. I kick him in the ribs. I leave him rocking his wound to sleep.

The trailers of performer row, large, with pop-outs and sliding glass doors, are dark. Four-by-four trucks with vanity plates wait quietly in front of each of them. Lawn chairs and barbecues, children's toys, are strewn about. I only saw the Afghani tumblers and Mexican fliers fighting in the midway. The rest, the Belgian seal act and the Chinese jugglers, must be hiding inside.

I haven't seen the clowns either. I wonder about Al.

Three cracks. Gunshots. I hit my knees. A crowd runs by, chasing a crying woman. Her torn shirt flaps behind her like a flag. Breasts bouncing, she tries to cover them, hold them still in her hands.

I recognize her. She's from the box office. She'll quit tomorrow. If she gets through tonight. I crawl to the shadows of the bigtop back door.

Behind me, the world explodes. M-80 in the dumpster. Dirt rains on my head. Laughter, then running feet. Then crackling heat. The yellow and white horse tent catches fire. I stand frozen. The smoke smells sweet. I take a few deep breaths, try to place the smell. Then a sharp pain sears my nose and throat. My lungs seize. The polypro rope from the horse tent is melting. Choking, eyes streaming, I stumble from the greasy fumes.

Lean my forehead against a cool sidepole. Breathe: In two, out three. In two, out three.

My breath is labored. Loud. It wheezes through my closing throat. I cover my nose and mouth uselessly with my tee-shirt.

As suddenly as it came, adrenaline drains from me. Its absence leaves me cold. I bend over my knees spitting bile, then stretch my arms overhead, expanding my lungs, straining for oxygen. Maybe God's punishing me. Maybe I'll suffocate. My head swims. I deserve to stop breathing, I want to stop breathing. I'm crashing. The rage is slipping. Gone. Guilt rushes in to replace it. I've become just like them. Like Jay. Like Pa. Maybe someone will come by and kill me. I couldn't be that lucky.

Horses gallop out of their burning stalls. Lou and the groom run behind, shooing them towards the slaughterhouse. They run panicked, are caught short by the yellow security fence. Whinnying, snorting, the horses kick at the fence, knock it down, run away from the circus.

If anyone is hurt, it's my fault. Everything destroyed is my fault. Oh God. Hands on hips, I walk in a circle, breath returning.

The horse tent burns slowly. Plastic-coated canvas melts from center to edge, heat wind billowing bits of blackened tent upwards. Live embers float on a warm current of air. Behind the tent, on boss row side, the wall of hay bales catches. Next to that, Tom's trailer.

Tammy's inside. I left her there alone. My intestines cramp.

I run towards flames. Dreamlike memories of familiar

sensations, another fire. Acrid smoke, black-ash-filled nostrils. Heat slapping my face.

A child's hiccuping sobs, choking. Face red, grimacing. Wailing, Tammy stands on the aluminum stairs, gripping Barbie. Ken forgotten in the muddy straw. I grab her around the waist. "It's okay, I'm here," I say. I huck her rigid body over my shoulder like a sidepole. Her screams deaden the brawling noises.

To the generator truck. I keep the shine of its metal walls square in my vision, all the while edging round the midway rumble. My hand cupped over Tammy's mouth, she quiets, but her hot tears fall on my knuckles, and her moist breath drips in my palm.

"It's alright, shh," I whisper to her. My voice is hoarse. Breathing still hurts.

Her little chest twitches with slowing sobs, and her ribs jounce painfully against my collarbone. She smells like chemical smoke and urine.

"We're almost there. We'll turn on the lights, and the bad men will go home, Honey-bunny," I whisper to her. She nods, like a good girl, her lips brushing against my fingers.

We are nearly at the gennie, nearly safe. I keep talking to her. "I know, shh. Your mama's gonna come and everything will be all right." I lie in a soft voice, so she'll stay quiet and calm.

"Hey!" A man stumbles into the corner of my vision.

Tammy startles. My right hand remembers its firm grip on wood. In a graceful half turn, outstretched arm a beautiful arc, soft elbows, pretty hands, I pirouette and the sledgehammer handle connects solidly with Bo's temple.

He falls bonelessly. I straddle his unconscious form. Nudge his thigh with my toe. His body responds without tension, like a dead thing. It shakes a bit, then settles again into an unnatural rest.

I put Tammy down. She stands next to my leg, hands wrapped around my knee. Staring at Bo.

A few more seconds pass, then I hold the back of my hand to his nostrils. The lot is surprisingly still, as if the battle quieted so Bo wouldn't wake up.

Warm moisture on my skin. He's still breathing, still alive.

I pull Tammy off my leg. I grab her shoulders and turn her around. "Give me a minute," I say.

Kneeling next to Bo's deaf ear, I whisper, "Is this the battle you wanted?"

He doesn't answer; I didn't expect him to. Anyhow, I know the answer already. He and I aren't so different. Just like me, he got what he asked for. No victims here.

The gennie hums to life. Klieg lights rip the cover off the fight. Tom steps out the generator truck, wiping soot off his face with a bandanna. Smiling to see Tammy safe.

"Go to your uncle." I push her gently. She runs to his widespread arms. He catches her, lifts her high, rubs noses with her.

"That's my good girl," he says.

Now Tahar leads his elephants through the well-lit lot. Balloo and Ivory trumpet impressively. The brawl goes into shock. Townies and roustabouts alike stop. Look up. Ivory rears. The townies beneath her massive feet scatter.

Bull hook behind Balloo's ear, Tahar commands, "Move up, Balloo. Move up, Ivory." They charge. Our attackers drop their weapons, jump over the fence, and disappear.

Roustabouts chase behind them, as if it was their victory and not the elephants', yelling. "That's right, motherfuckers! Chickenshit!" They've won. The townies are run off. The roustabouts bang the security fence with sledgehammer handles. Hit fists on chests, slap backs. Strut with arms overhead. Adrenaline still pumping.

But I feel no triumph. My high's already been replaced with a painful emptiness. My hands are sticky; drying blood turns rusty on my palms. They're itchy from someone else's hair tangled in my fingers.

Behind me, Tom rocks Tammy. Her legs straddle his hip, his arms loop securely around her waist, her head droops on his shoulder. My arms feel empty. I catch Tammy's eye, and she buries her face in her uncle's shoulder. I'm sick with myself. I'm so empty and sick and cold, I wish I were dead.

"Your trailer burned," I tell Tom.

"I know."

"Where'll you sleep?"

One hand supporting Tammy, he fishes a silver flask from his hip. Unscrews it with his teeth. "Don't worry about us, Mat. You look like shit."

"I feel like shit." I think about hitting Bo. Breaking heads. I wonder how Tammy sees me now. I held her with these filthy hands.

We join the other circus folk wandering through the ruined lot. Picking up scraps, dropping them. Glass and plastic crunches under our heels. Concessionaires cluck over the damage done, the money lost. A command of "Every mother's son!" and they put their shoulders to righting an overturned snack wagon. The box-office betty leans against the entrance tent, clutching her torn shirt closed. She shivers. An electrician taps her shoulder. She falls at his feet.

Tom fingers an L-shaped rip in the sidewall. I turn my back to him, face the mess.

"What would you say if I told you this was my fault?"

Tom waits a bit before answering. Then, "I'd say you're talking crazy."

"No, it is."

"Ah, Mat." He hands me his half-empty hip flask. I drink and hang on to it.

Tom doesn't seem to mind. He just says, "Done is done."

Down performer row, the Flying Cordovas duct-tape a tarp over their pickup truck's broken windshield. We pass Tom's Citation. Fumes from melted upholstery hang in the air.

Tattoo Lou and Jay find each other in front of the burnt horse tent. White fire extinguisher foam coats the hay bales. Jay folds Lou in his arms.

Tammy snuffles, asleep in Tom's arms. I don't belong near children. She could've died. It would've been my fault. I don't know what disgusts me more, my guilt or my self-pity.

"Insurance'll cover it," he says.

Shit. I light a Lucky and wonder how I'll live.

"I started the fight." Tom opens his mouth, but I hold up my hand. "Listen, I was so angry. I went to Joe's. I wanted something to happen."

Tom puts his hand on my shoulder. "This has been brewing a long time, Mat."

Jay comforts Lou, strokes her hair, kisses her forehead. She cries comfortably, safely, against his chest.

I'm tired.

"I want to die," I tell Tom. He takes my elbow and leads me away from the horse tent.

*   *   *

We stop in front of the elephants. Tahar's already chained them for the night.

"They saved the day," Tom says.

"Yeah." I just want to die, God.

"Really powerful beasts."

"Yeah." Please, God? I'm fading away.

Ivory rocks against her shackle, Tom rocks his sleeping niece.

"You remember when Ivory pulled the truck out the mud?" Tom speaks from far away. If he wasn't holding my elbow, I couldn't hear him. "That's hard, moving a truck. Remember that?"

I nod. I remember that move. Moose River Bend, a nothing town. Population 300. We set up in a cleared hayfield, then it rained steady for three days and nights. The field turned to mud and the tent truck sank in to its axle. The Deere was useless because it got stuck too. Tom finally got Tahar to hook Ivory up to the truck and haul it to the road.

Tom juts his chin at Ivory's shackle, a small iron ring connected by a thin chain to a stake. "If she can pull a truck out the mud, can't she pull that stake out the dirt?"

I nod.

"You know why elephants rock like that?"

I wait. I watch his mouth for the answer. Tammy shifts in his arms. Ivory sways. My mind replays fires. Trailers burn over and over.

Finally he answers himself. "Comfort. If she didn't she'd go crazy."

I shift my weight from foot to foot. "It don't help me."

Tom laughs. Then, serious again, "Mat, listen to me. Ivory doesn't know how strong she is. She doesn't know she could escape. She got chained up when she was little and weak. Too little to pull up the stake. Now she believes she still can't. She doesn't even try. That's how training is done. Get them while they're young." He brushes a hair from my eyes, and nearly breaks my heart.

Five A.M. The sky just beginning to gray. I find Al passed out behind the steam tables and tuck Calico Bear into his arms. Kiss the top of his head. He doesn't stir. Jay and Lou, Tom, Tante, and everyone else, are safe asleep. Warm under covers and waiting for morning. Not me. I walk past the dark sleepers, the dark trailers, and say goodbye to each of their doors. I can imagine them curled in their bunks; each face is clearly seared on my tired brain. They've marked me, as sure and deep as lovers carving initials in a tree. They'll split up, move on, die, but I'll never be able to smooth over their memory. I can leave them, but they'll never leave me.

Outside the yellow security fence, I face east and stick my thumb west. I walk backwards along the highway. I'm running away from the circus to join the real world.

For a moment, everything looks so sharp, so clear. Every pebble in the road, every blade of grass. Then my chest splinters and cracks. My eyes fill, and I begin to cry. Tears spill over and soften the world. I wipe my bloody hands across my wet cheeks, scrub them clean and dry on my tee-shirt. I hold a quivering drop on the end of my finger. The rising sun glints through it, makes it sparkle like a rhinestone.

Tante says only the women whose eyes have been washed clean with tears see clearly. When I'm done crying, my eyes will be clearer than anyone's. I'm gonna hike till I hit the ocean, wade right in to that salt water. Then I'm gonna look through my new clean eyes for the next good thing.